REVENGE OF THE TWO-HEADED POETRY MONSTER

REVENGE OF THE TWO-HEADED POETRY MONSTER

100 Poems of Horror and Wonder

by Michael McCarty and Mark McLaughlin

Revenge of the Two-Headed Poetry Monster

© 2013 by Michael McCarty and Mark McLaughlin
published 2013 by Elektrik Milk Bath Press

Cover Art and Interior Artwork © by Mark McLaughlin

Published by Elektrik Milk Bath Press. For information, please contact Elektrik Milk Bath Press, P.O. Box 833223, Richardson, TX 75083.

www.elektrikmilkbathpress.com

Poems copyright © Michael McCarty and Mark McLaughlin. Illustrations copyright © Mark McLaughlin.

All rights reserved.

No part of this book may be used or reproduced in any manner whatsoever without written permission, except in the case of brief quotations embodied in critical articles or reviews.

ISBN 978-0-9894616-0-3

Contents

INTRODUCTION:
No Bawdy Rhymes for Nantucket in THIS Book of Poetry, Thank You Very Much!
by Professor Artemis Theodore LaGungo

BLESSINGS & BLASPHEMIES
by Mark McLaughlin

1. Cinema Diabolique	15
2. Big is Beautiful	17
3. Electric Charity Begins at Home	18
4. The Storyteller Out of Time	19
5. What the Sorceress with a Sweet Tooth Had to Say to the Angry Mob Before They Cut Out Her Tongue	20
6. Cleopatrick	21
7. Rotted Hearts Ought Not to Pulse	22

MONSTERS, MADMEN & MIDNIGHT MOVIES
by Michael McCarty

8. Psycho Woman in My Shower	25
9. Frankenfrog	26
10. Ich	27
11. The Troll of Madison County	28
12. Son of Wyatt Earp Battles the Aztec Mummy (with Cindy McCarty)	29
13. Requiem	30
14. The Road to Hell	31
15. The Old House on the Corner (with Terrie Leigh Relf)	32
16. Making Out with Kali	34
17. Dangerous	35
18. Dusk (with R.L. Fox)	36
19. The Pet Exorcist	37
20. Frosty the Serial Killer Snowman	39
21. My Cannibal Girlfriend	40
22. Of Thee I Sing	41
23. The Word	42
24. Somebody's Knocking	44

MONSTER METAL: NECRO-PUNK-ROCK ANTHEM No. 1
by Mark McLaughlin and Michael McCarty

25. Orange Demon in My Brain   46

THE SPIDERWEB TREE
by Mark McLaughlin

26. The Spiderweb Tree   49
27. Hansel & Gristle   50
28. Ratpunzel   51
29. Horror House of Thumb   52
30. Saved from a Grizzly Demise   53
31. Wicked Queen   56
32. Ashley   57
33. Joe White   60
34. Loved Her, Hated Him   61
35. Kiss   62
36. Stalked   63

MOTHER GOOSE, COOKED TO PERFECTION
by Michael McCarty

37. Zombie Jack Spratt   66
38. Jack Be Dinner   67
39. Old Mother Hubbard's Kennel of Blood   68

COSMIC HORRORS, UNIVERSAL PICTURES: MYTHOS MONSTERS STAR IN CLASSIC HORROR FILMS
by Mark McLaughlin

40. Nyarlathenstein   70
41. Cthulhu's Daughter   71
42. Pickman's Werewolf   72
43. The Colour from the Blasted Lagoon   73

SLIMY CREATURES FROM OUTER SPACE
by Michael McCarty

Introduction	77
44. Alien Prisoner (with Sandy DeLuca)	78
45. Crop Circles	81
46. Cute, Cuddly Creatures from Another Planet	83
47. Gone Hollywood	84
48. Not One of Us	85
49. Illegal Aliens	86
50. Area 51, Where are You?	87
51. The Others (with Sandy DeLuca)	88
52. Alien Anal Probe	89
53. MIB	90
54. MIB II	91
55. War of the Worlds	92
56. It Came from Uranus	93
57. Alien Autopsy	94
58. Lights from the Sky	95
59. The Slimy Monster from Outer Space	96

SPEAKING PARTS: FRANKENSTEIN'S MONSTER RESTITCHED AS A BODY OF VERSE
by Mark McLaughlin

60. I Am the Monster's Naval	99
61. I Am the Monster's Heart	100
62. I Am the Monster's Penis	101
63. I Am the Monster's Fifth Kidney	102
64. I Am the Monster's Right Knee	103
65. I Am the Monster's Left Ear	104
66. I Am the Monster's Bottom Lip	105
67. I Am the Monster's Pinky	106
68. I Am the Monster's Stomach	107
69. I Am the Monster's Hazel Eye	108
70. I Am the Monster's Thumb	109
71. I Am the Monster's Sphincter	110
72. I Am the Monster's Brain	111

THE VAMPIRE SEXTETTE
by Michael McCarty

73. Beyond the Moonlight (with Terrie Leigh Relf) — 115
74. Succubus — 116
75. Vampire's Kiss — 117
76. Vegas Undead — 118
77. Sex with a Vampire — 119
78. Television — 120

MONSTER METAL: NECRO-PUNK-ROCK ANTHEM No. 2
by Mark McLaughlin and Michael McCarty

79. Zombie Insomniacs — 122

YOUR HANDY OFFICE GUIDE TO CORPORATE MONSTERS, Part 1:
KISS-UPS, BROWN-NOSERS & OTHER OFFICE ABSURDITIES
by Mark McLaughlin

80. The Enthusiraptor — 125
81. The Fumigorgon — 126
82. The Normitron — 127
83. The Smiling Gladhander — 128
84. The Waffler — 129
85. The Spittylicker — 130
86. The Blabberblort — 131
87. The Potbellied Smirkleflab — 132
88. The Zitastrophee — 133
89. The Finicky Foofoo — 134
90. The Screaming Snotty — 135
91. The Caterwauler — 136

YOUR HANDY OFFICE GUIDE TO CORPORATE MONSTERS, Part 2: CREATURES FROM BEYOND THE CUBICLE
by Michael McCarty and Mark McLaughlin

92. The Backstabbing Narkalope	138
93. The Slothazoid	139
94. The Belligerent Brag-Hag	140
95. The Office Oddball	141
96. The Cheerful Chirper	142
97. The Brainless Dawdler	143
98. The Snore Bore	144
99. The Mirrorgazing Megalomaniac	145
100. The Nicotine Nightmare	146

ACKNOWLEDGMENTS

DEDICATIONS

Michael would like to thank: Cindy McCarty, Latte the Bunny, Bev, Gerald, Steve McCarty, Angela, Cathy and David Leonard, Ron Stewart, Terrie Leigh Relf, Charlee Jacob, Teri Jacobs, Bobbi Sinha-Morey, Sandy DeLuca, Sherry Decker, R.L. Fox, Ray Bradbury, Edgar Allan Poe, Joe McKinney, Mel Piff, Elvira, T.S. Elliott, Rain Graves, Tyree, Camilla Bowman, The Amazing Kreskin, the other Michael McCarty, Paul from Barnes & Noble, The Source Bookstore, The Book Rack, Brian Kronfeld, Jean B, Linnea Q, The Melaines, and of course, my fellow dreamer, Mark.

Mark would like to thank: Michael S., Michael and Cindy McC., Pamela, Greg, Angela, Jody, Kyra, Pitch, Charlee, Mel, Jean, Tang, and Bob at The Book Rack. Thanks to the B-movie directors, writers, performers and folks-in-monster-suits whose work has thrilled me over the years. Thanks, too, to the fictional characters who have inspired me with their tomfoolery: Godzilla, Mothra, Cthulhu, Gamera, Scooby Doo, and those nasty villains who would have gotten away with it, if it weren't for those meddling kids and that blasted dog.

INTRODUCTION:
No Bawdy Rhymes for Nantucket in THIS Book of Poetry, Thank You Very Much!
by Professor Artemis Theodore LaGungo

    Horror authors and frequent collaborators Michael McCarty and Mark McLaughlin have written about my adventures many times over the years. So when the boys asked me to write the introduction to their latest book of poetry, I readily agreed.
    I regard these fine fellows as marvelous friends—and excellent customers, since both regularly visit my little shoppe of horrific goodies, *Professor LaGungo's Exotic Artifacts & Assorted Mystic Collectibles*.
    McLaughlin and McCarty are both connoisseurs of the unearthly and the bizarre. McLaughlin buys all his ancient Lemurian artifacts from me. In fact, I'm the one who sold him the Time Machine of Terror!, which he uses to explore the dimension of horror movies and scary television shows. What, you didn't know that horror movies and scary television shows had their own dimension? It's right around the corner from the dimension of people who haven't been born yet. Surely you know about *that* dimension, since you used to live there... before you were born, of course.
    When McCarty visits my shoppe, he purchases iron maidens, spine-stretching racks, maces, thumb-screws and other handy implements of torture. I'm sure he only uses them for decorative purposes. Well, *fairly* sure. It's hard to imagine such a nice young fellow using such awful instruments of pain on others.... Maybe he only uses them on people who really *deserve* to be tortured, like slowpoke waiters who take a long time bringing me my

order when I'm really hungry, or stubborn supermarket cashiers who won't honor my coupons just because they're a few years past the expiration date.

Please note: This is a classy book of poetry, with no uncouth rhymes for Nantucket to be found amidst its pages. But what WILL you find inside this book, you ask?

In this book, you will find ten-thousand mental demons, unleashed by McLaughlin and McCarty to destroy the brains of the human race! You, the reader, will experience the torments of the damned, and those torments will grow even more tormentulous with the turning of every page. Now, some of you may say that tormentulous is not a word—but once your soul has been shredded to weensy bits by all the tormentulous terrors to be found in this book…. THEN you will truly know just how truly tormentulous a torment can get!

Having said all that, I leave you to the tender mercies of McLaughlin and McCarty. But before I go, I encourage each and every one of you to visit my shoppe and buy a few mystic collectibles for your home. Wouldn't your living room look altogether more adventurous and stylish with a stuffed two-headed crocodile hanging by sturdy copper chains over the entertainment center? Shouldn't your guest room feature an ancient Egyptian altar for worshipping Anubis? After all, what guest room is complete without one?

I shall now finish this introduction by saying: Enjoy! Enjoy shopping at *Professor LaGungo's Exotic Artifacts & Assorted Mystic Collectibles*!

Oh, and when you get a chance… read this book.

Thank you.

BLESSINGS & BLASPHEMIES
by Mark McLaughlin

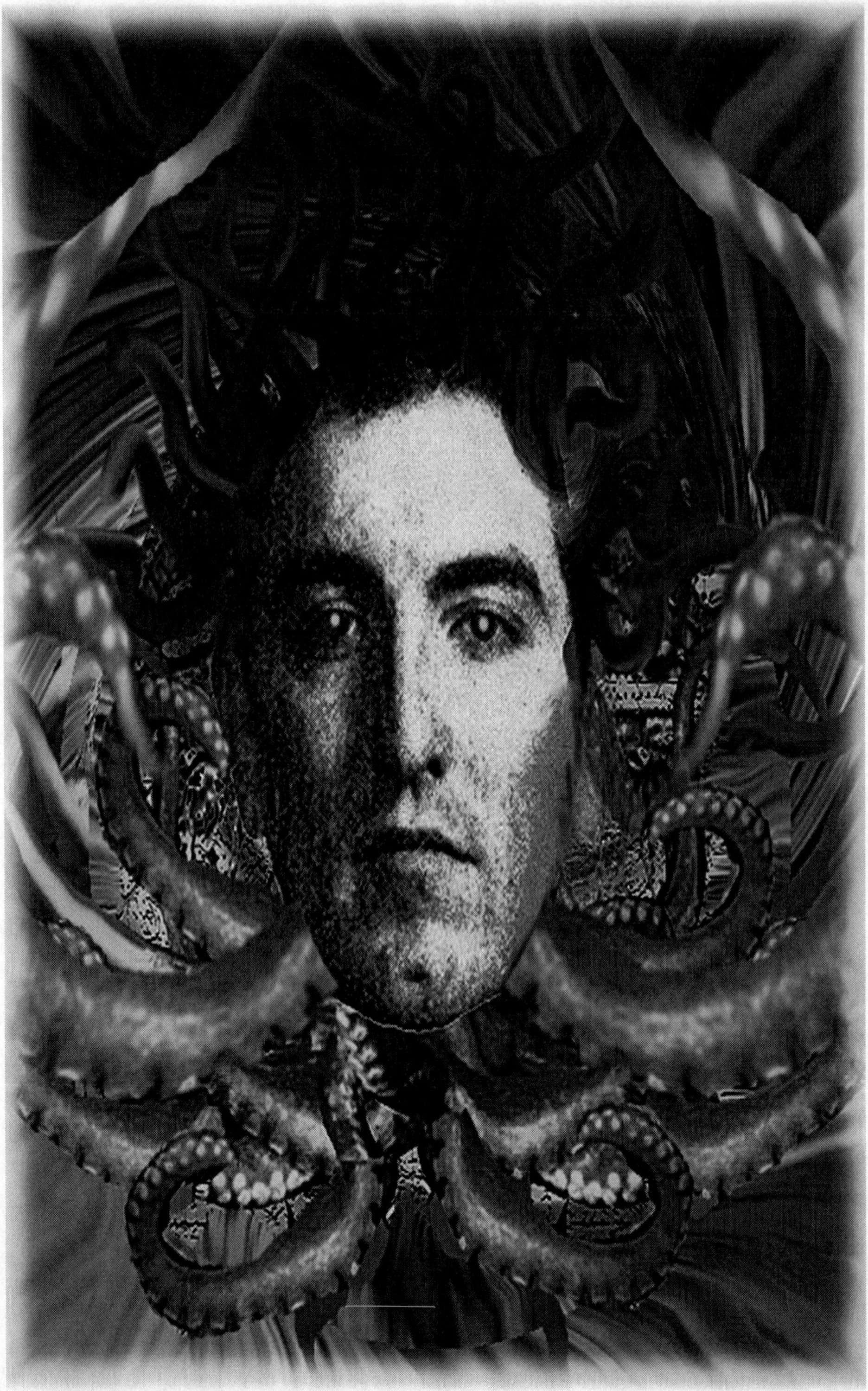

1.

Cinema Diabolique

WATCH THE SCREEN

Behold:
A scrawl in blood and crushed insects on the door
Hidebound books and shards of cold black glass
A robed crone whispers to a devil-cat gone mad
Gray flesh flaking from bones as soft as Hell
Locked rooms alive with whimpering (so sad)
Puddle-eyed dollies tear into morgue-slab treats
Lightning rips a black silk sky to shreds
Shrieks of pain or perhaps delight (so hard to tell)
Dead hands lovingly stroke decaying heads

YOU WERE A FOOL TO COME HERE
AND SIT FRIENDLESS IN THE GLOATING DARK
DO NOT GLANCE AT THOSE SEATED NEARBY
YOU'RE SIMPLY HERE FOR GHASTLY FUN
SO TRY NOT TO SCREAM AS THE EXIT SIGNS
WINK OUT ONE BY ONE

The tale must be told:
Eye-sockets filled with silver scorpions
Bubbling spittle drips from rancid tongues
A puffy corpse swirls down a midnight creek
Baby-fat candles flicker in an icy breeze
(No one will ever know the awful truth)
Hairless bats fly across the moon in a blur
Wicked things cavort with a pulsing freak
A gaunt beast picks bits of shroud from its teeth
An unloved child seals a pact as fly-wings whir

ALLOW THE NIGHT'S BLACK SOUL
TO LOVINGLY CONSOLE YOU
WITH IMAGES OF SOOTHING DEATH
VIPER-FANGS PIERCE YOUR BRAIN

DOWN TO ITS LIVING CORE
YOU FEEL THE VENOMOUS THRILL
AND PLEAD FOR MORE

At last:
Zombies tear down the rusted iron gates
Cruel lips suck down intestines like spaghetti
The smiling doctor fills a syringe with acid
(A cure far worse than any mere disease)
Demons babble with barbed-wire ecstasy
Glowing green clouds descend on the city
A skinless grin and rows of sharp incisors
That which feasts on fear has found a home
The full moon bursts like a sac of baby spiders
Words on the screen roll on and on and on and–

HELL ERUPTS AROUND AND WITHIN YOU
ALL YOU ARE IS SATAN'S TASTY MEAT
DO NOT CRY MY HORRID DARLING
FOR SOON YOU WILL BE UNBORN
AND A BRAND-NEW PATRON
WILL TAKE YOUR COMFY SEAT
SIT STILL AS GAUNT USHERS
WITH LIPS AND HANDS OF FLAME
MELT AWAY YOUR SOUL
TO FLAVOR THE POPCORN

2.

Big is Beautiful

There she is: the model
who turned the catwalk
into the fatwalk.
Her name is Zazza Opulchka
and she is seven feet tall
and weighs four-hundred
and eighty-nine pounds.
They say she grew up in
a peaceful village in a valley
behind a nuclear power plant
in the Republic of Krezda.
She starts each glamorous day
with a high-protein breakfast of
fried eggs and roasted suckling pig
and exercises by tearing down
warehouses with her bare hands.
She's surprisingly agile and can
run seventy miles an hour without
sweating a drop. She is beautiful
in her own special, relentless way,
like a killer shark, or a tornado,
or a comet hurling through space.
She has the prettiest eyes, and such
wonderfully thick blonde hair.
Fashion designers love her
because she's so different from
all the other models. These days,
teenage girls everywhere are eating
ice cream, bacon, candy bars and
pork chops, so they can be big,
powerful and alluring, just like
Zazza Opulchka. Sure, the camera
adds ten pounds, but that's
just not enough.

3.

Electric Charity Begins at Home

My dainty duck, it was bad of you, wrong of you,
wrong of you, bad of you, to do such horrid things.
Why, my pet? Why did so many people have to die,
and through the use of such a rambunctious array
of power tools? But it's too late, far too late now.
You must be punished, you know. So follow me,
my tender kitten, to the seat of horror and dishonor.
Let me buckle you in. Not too tight? Good. Now,
where's that on/off switch? You deserve to die
and so you must. One little flick and you shall fry,
ending your psychotic shenanigans. Serial killers:
why must they always seek me out to both love
and punish them? Well, here we go! Cheerio,
aloha, adieu, sayonara, and arrivederci. In short:
goodbye. Aaaah, once again, the horrid weight
has been lifted! Now I can get on with my life,
and you, my honeysuckle horror, can get on
with your death.

4.

The Storyteller Out of Time

His love of horror
Pushed his reader's minds
Long light-years into endless voids
Of night. His verbal fangs shot
Venom into willing brains, and
Evil dwelled in yarns of
Cosmic fright. He made folks shudder!
Rugged he was not, but still
Adventure was his bread and eldritch butter.
For tales as grim and icy as the tomb,
There was, and is, no greater voice of doom.

5.

What the Sorceress with a Sweet Tooth Had to Say to the Angry Mob Before They Cut Out Her Tongue

No! Stop! I need my evil tongue
to address my dark master, Asmodeus,
and to taste pudding. I love pudding.
How am I supposed to enjoy my pudding
without a tongue? Stop trying to grab
my tongue with those tongs. How many
other sorceresses have you used those
tongue-tongs on? Do you wash them
between sorceresses? I really doubt it.
While I've still got a tongue in my head,
I hereby place a curse on all of you.
Even those in the back. May all of your
descendants from this day forth be
tongue-tied fools, never speaking up,
never getting what they want. But they
shall get what they deserve, and that's
nothing. No money. No love.
No future. No hope.
And no dessert.

6.

Cleopatrick

Red hair, freckles, overbite, and that's not all:
he's different in another, special way.
Not quite right, but far from wrong.
Slanted panther-eyes and sultry curves.
A subtle sibilance upon his tongue.
Lotus breath and dusty, musky pits.
He works at Loco Video (camp DVDs,
some porn, some foreign crap),
but in his mind life's too B.C. for words:
stone corridors, misshapen deities,
ferocious hieroglyphics haunt his dreams.
He hisses the name ISIS to the disks –
breathes truth into their files, along with death
and cold , relentless time.
Soon, all the shows reveal epiphanies:
each scene tells of a smirking universe
that doesn't care. Cycles within cycles swirl
with merciless precision. Wind and sand
are all that really matter. Those who see
these DVDs turn mummy in their minds,
their thoughts all desert-dry. How sad,
how mad. Our priestly, beastly boy
refuses sleep. He stares up at the moon
and tries to cry.

7.

Rotted Hearts Ought Not to Pulse

Boom-boom, boom-boom, boom-boom.
Rotted hearts ought not to pulse, but this one did,
that rainy, wretched Sunday afternoon.
It pulsed and pulsed in a rusty box
hidden under rags and broken bones
in a shadowed, cobwebbed corner
of the living room of the living dead
in a horror house of endless pain
in a phantom world of oily clouds
and screaming hills and steaming lakes
of curdled blood in a realm of endless tears,
falling like wretched Sunday rain
on screaming hills and a horror house
of endless pain, in which could be found
the living room of the living dead,
in the corner of which, under rags
and broken bones, in a rusted box,
there pulsed and pulsed a rotted heart –
yes, this one did, though it really ought not.
Boom-boom, boom-boom, boom-boom.

MONSTERS, MADMEN & MIDNIGHT MOVIES
by Michael McCarty

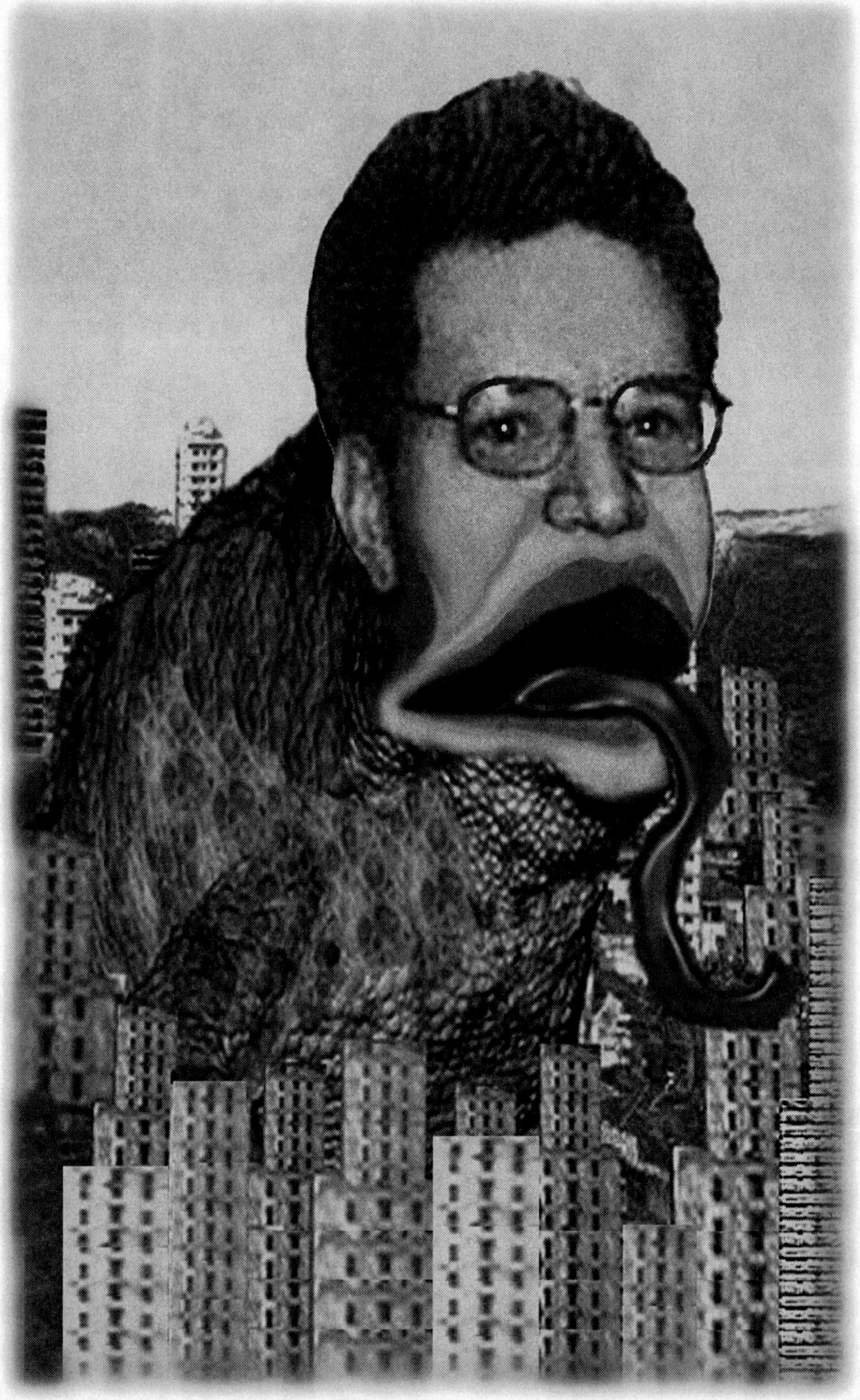

8.

Psycho Woman in My Shower

There's a psycho woman in my shower.
No, I'm not talking about
Janet Leigh.
It's my neighbor.

She came over to borrow some sugar—
the next thing I knew,
she stripped
and started taking a shower.

That was last week.

She's been showering
for so long,
her skin is
way beyond prunes

I don't mind being neighborly,
But now she's starting to scare me.

9.

Frankenfrog

little green froggy in the middle of the bog
sittin' and spittin' like a big ol' hog

one day a demented doctor took
the lil' critter from his swampy nook

did lab tests from old horror books
dramatically altering our hero's looks

frankenfrog returned to his favorite swampland
with bolts in his neck that'd scare ayn rand

end of the poem is very sad
nobody visits poor frankenfrog's pad

10.

Ich

ich
white
shiny death
that eats away my fish

poor
little fishy
swims around losing
chunky smelly pieces of itself

i
pick
up the fish
and the ich gets on my fingertips

the
ich is
hungry and
starts eating my hand, my arm, my face—

11.

The Troll of Madison County

If you're gonna have bridges,
you've gotta have trolls.

And that's what I do.
That's my big starring role.

Ugly thing with no soul,
with one mission and goal.

So pay me my toll
or end up in a hole.

All the clever goats know:
cross a bridge, pay the troll.

12.

Son of Wyatt Earp Battles the Aztec Mummy
(with Cindy McCarty)

First there was Jesse James Meets Frankenstein's Daughter
Then came Billy the Kid Vs. Dracula
Now – from the producers who brought you Bloodsucking Demons from Mars
And Oliver Blaine, director of The Bee-Girls and The Bee-Girls from Beyond –
Prepare yourself for Son of Wyatt Earp Battles the Aztec Mummy
Featuring world-renowned wrestler/actor Big-Bear Breckenridge

One rose from a Mexican tomb to terrify the world ... on a really low budget
The other rode into Tombstone, Texas to restore order to the town
Fate brought the two together for one unforgettable night
It's the Wild West meets South of the Border
See it with someone who's not embarrassed to rent such schlock
Thank God it's only a B-movie ... coming soon to a video store near you

13.

Requiem

She who understands light
must understand darkness.
Hallows is the labyrinth,
the path to the underworld.

Hallows Eve is the day
we sing a sad requiem
for those confined to
the Land of the Dead.

The Goddess of the Dead
cries her burning tears
as she descends to her
underground netherworld.

The Goddess barely hears
the melancholy melodies
of the requiem performed
from above.

She
sleeps
during the grim
Change of Seasons.

Dark sky and dark night
give way to light.
It is time for the rebirth
of a new moon and a new year.

14.

The Road to Hell

the highway is one
long stretched-out graveyard
intestines splattered down
the middle of the road
hung bodies swing back
and forth from the overpass
the median strip is made
of stegosaurus back-bones
bloody heads are posted
on top of exit signs
the off-ramps all lead
to eternal damnation

15.

The Old House on the Corner
by Terrie Leigh Relf & Michael McCarty

It is cold. . .near winter,
and the house on the corner
cloaks itself within a silent shroud,
bows to the night. . .to the cold stark
night, while I wait beneath the bougainvillea
for a sign, any sign...

I knew he was still alive
hiding somewhere
deep inside the walls, the cellar
the attic, and so

I search through each and every room,
but he is nowhere.

While I attempt to fall asleep,
his face, his scent, haunt me still.
He must be alive;
this I know is true,
although buried beneath
the town's cemetery
in a grave not his own.

The clock strikes twelve,
and I measure each and every chime,
remember how we loved. . .
when the slightest touch
made our bodies shiver,
despair and grief, so very far
from our minds.

Is the window open?
I feel a cool whisper on my
cheek, and it grows colder
as I turn toward the fluttering

curtains, realize the window
is closed.

There is an icy caress
gentle upon my breasts, my neck. . .
and the candle on the nightstand,
its flame burns then flickers,
stoked by his ghostly breath.

16.

Making Out with Kali

Kali is naked
and standing in front of me
all eight arms embrace me
four of them for pleasure
four of them for pain
when I see her necklace
made of human skulls
I go limp

Kali is singing
sweet melodies of death
I love watching
all four of her
tattooed breasts
sway back and forth
and between her legs is a
dark, inviting place

Kali is a vengeful goddess
full of cruel and evil ways
a blood-sucking bitch
who enjoys tossing heads
but when I'm on top of her
with her purple tongue
inside my mouth
all I feel is love

17.

Dangerous

It's dangerous to dream about you,
dangerous, I know.
But in the tender moonlight
with the stars shining bright,
it seems like the right thing to do.

It's dangerous for me to stray,
more dangerous to stay.
But in the embrace of the night
with your eyes oh-so-bright,
it seems like the right thing to do.

It's dangerous to love you,
dangerous, it's true.
As we lie in your tomb,
I won't think about doom.
It seems like the right thing to do.

18.

Dusk
(with R.L. Fox)

It's been thirty days now
since I last fed my desire.
My head was spinning,
my blood was on fire.
The moon propelled me
into the streets of the night.

Some call me immoral.
Some call me dangerous.
Some men hate me,
others are envious.
It doesn't really matter
when the moon shines bright.

Some women come easy,
others must be convinced.
When they fall under my spell
they have no defense,
waiting for the new moon's light.

It doesn't matter what time it is,
when the moon shines anew.
It doesn't matter what your name is,
because this much is true:
you're my prisoner of the night
and your skin pierces easily
from my sharp bite.

19.

The Pet Exorcist

the pet exorcist
a priest/ veterinarian
casts evil spirits
out of household pets

he's seen it all:
the goldfish from the river Styx
the canary that wouldn't die
the dog who licked himself

then one evening
he received a call
about the most malevolent
of all evil spirits –

the kitty from hell
the feline from hades
the kitten from limbo-land
the tomcat from the inferno
it was one bad pussy

this tabby was spitting up
fiery furballs
and chasing
a never-ending ball of yarn

the pet exorcist
blessed the mouser
with holy water
a foolish mistake
kitties don't like
getting wet

hissing and spitting
clawing and biting
the enraged hellcat tossed

the pet exorcist around
like a cheap toy mouse
the priest made tracks
out of that house

barely escaping
with his life
he gave up that gig
for a safer career
last I heard
he's a nuclear demolitions expert

20.

Frosty the Serial Killer Snowman

Frosty the Serial Killer Snowman
is a crafty, vicious soul
with a bent crackpipe and a shiny axe
and a heart of blackest coal.

There must have been bad magic
in that vampire cape they found,
for when they wrapped it 'round his neck
he began to slice folks down.

Frosty the Serial Killer Snowman
loves a jolly Christmas slay!
He's an evil joe and the hookers know
he'll come after them someday.

Down in the village
with a chainsaw in his hand,
he runs here and there, all around the square,
screaming, "Catch me if you can!"

Frosty the Serial Killer Snowman
had to hurry on his way.
He may flee the law and the warm spring thaw
but he'll kill us all someday!

21.

My Cannibal Girlfriend

It ain't easy dating
a cannibal girlfriend.
When you kiss her
good night
you can taste
someone else.

It ain't easy dining with
a cannibal girlfriend.
You make her dinner –
a bloody-red steak –
and she says,
"Gross! How long has this been
dead?"

It ain't easy making love to
a cannibal girlfriend.
Are you just another
piece of meat?
Is she imagining you
with butter
melting down your back?

It ain't easy marrying
a cannibal girlfriend.
Your matrimony ceremony
is a strange combo of
wedding, funeral and
all-you-can-eat buffet.

No, it ain't easy living with
a cannibal girlfriend.
Sometimes love just bites.

22.

Of Thee I Sing

Who'd have believed
the greatest nation in the world,
America, would fall to dust?
Once so alive, it is now extinct.
The survivors wander this sprawling graveyard,
wishing they were dead –
seeking food, shelter, salvation,
finding nothing.
The lucky ones lie dead on windswept streets.
Their dull, staring eyes have turned
away from their own country,
toward the nation of God.

23.

The Word

The Word
The perfect word
The one that makes
My Creative Writing classmates curl up under their desks in utter shame.

The Word
The intellectual word
The one that makes
My writing teacher say,
"Boy, he writes better than Stephen King and John Irving combined."

The Word
The commercial word
The one that's turned
Into a novel
Which is turned into a film
Which is turned into a TV series
Which has reruns on cable from late night to early morning.

The Word
The powerful word
The one that makes you feel
Like someone just squeezed your balls in a vise
And you scream at the top of your lungs but no one can save you.

The Word
The immortal word
The one that makes
Me a god among men
As I go down in literary history
And have celebrity parties where illiterates are called boogerbutts.

The Word
The saving word
The one that gives
Food to the homeless

And makes
Bomb-makers stop making bombs
Junkies put down their drug needles
And flesh-eating zombies stop eating the brains of stupid victims.

Billions of words
Floating in my brain
Enough to drive a man insane –

Which one do I choose?
Which one do I use?

24.

Somebody's Knocking

Somebody's knocking,
don't answer the door.
It might just be a looter, looking for more.
Whatever you do,
Don't let him in.
It's a big-city riot
and your life's gonna end.

Somebody's knocking,
don't answer the door.
It might just be Jesus, Son of the Lord.
Whatever you do,
don't let Him in.
It's the Second Coming
and mankind's gonna end.

Somebody's knocking,
don't answer the door.
It might just be Satan, foul to the core.
Whatever you do,
don't let Him in.
It's the Apocalypse
and the world's gonna end.

MONSTER METAL: NECRO-PUNK-ROCK ANTHEM No. 1
by Mark McLaughlin and Michael McCarty

25.

Orange Demon in My Brain

Secrets inked on ancient vellum –
terror in my cerebellum –
if you see the Devil, tell him:
something has escaped from Hell
and lives inside my head.
Somehow it has cast a spell
to make my brain undead!

Orange demon in my brain –
he calls to me!
Orange demon shall remain –
he crawls to me!
All I do is think about him.
I could never live without him!

Now I have a brain of madness –
never more shall I know sadness –
evil fills my soul with gladness!
Fantasies of orange fire
make the world seem dead and dull.
Wicked visions of desire
lurk within my haunted skull!

Orange demon in my brain –
 he calls to me!
Orange demon shall remain –
 he crawls to me!
All I do is think about him.
I could never live without him!

THE SPIDERWEB TREE
by Mark McLaughlin

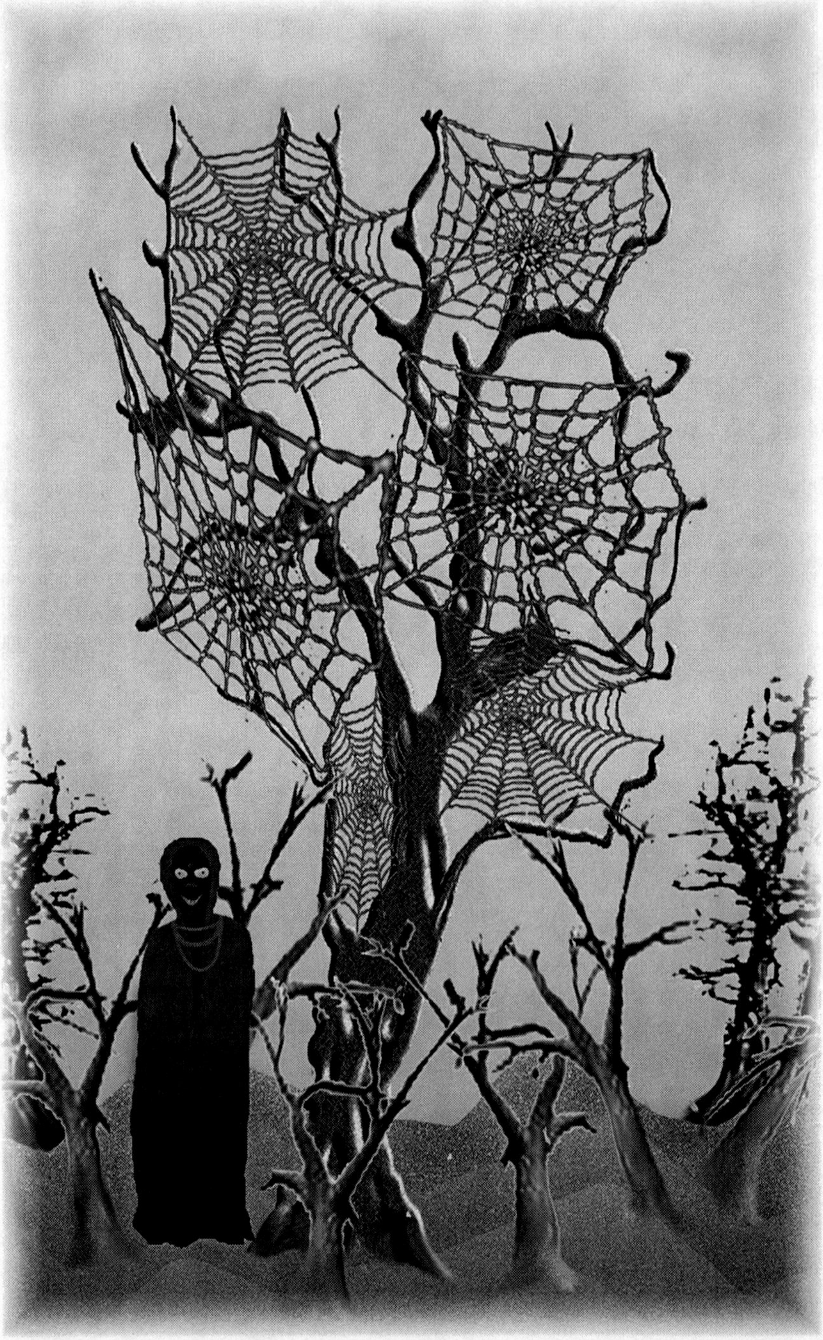

26.

The Spiderweb Tree

The oak tree is dead,
long dead. And the branches
are filled with spiderwebs.
Makes you wonder. After all,
spiders don't travel in packs.
Of course, there's a swamp
not too far away – thousands
of tasty bugs in a swamp.
The wind must blow the dinner
into those webs. But still,
that's an awful lot of spiders
for just one tree.

I've seen some funny tracks
on the road near that tree.
Tires. Wagon-wheels. Hooves.
Paw-prints as big as hands.
Boot-prints as wee as peanuts.
Slimy snail-trails a foot wide.
Strange comings and goings.
Spiders have eight eyes each.
They see what's going on.
Not that it matters. You won't
get a word out of them.

Such a baffling tree. But it's
lovely in winter – especially
at midnight, when delicate
crystals, caught in the lacework,
shimmer like playful stars
in the moonlight. A sight
like that both soothes and
excites me. I can stare at it
for hours. It looks just how
love feels. Or perhaps
death.

27.

Hansel & Gristle

Brother Hansel was a plump, jolly,
blue-eyed scamp in lederhosen.
Sister Gristle was a blubbery chunk
of fat, sinews and oily cartilage.
Oh, the adventures they had!
Once, they found an old road
that wandered past a dead oak tree
with branches draped in spiderwebs.
That road led into the deep, dark
woods, where they came across
a rainbow-colored candy-house
and its owner, a hideous witch
who tried to enslave poor Gristle
and eat chubby little Hansel.
But they tricked her, you bet!
Hansel held down the witch
while Gristle stuffed some of
her own greasy, disgusting body
into the witch's mouth.
The old hag choked to death
on her own vomit.
Hansel and Gristle stayed
at the house for three months,
eating it down to the ground.
The next week, they captured
one of the Three Little Pigs
and barbecued him.

28.

Ratpunzel

"Ratpunzel, Ratpunzel, let down your tail,
so I may climb thy hairy trail." This
the Prince sang, and soon from the window
swang yards and yards of scaly, sinewy,
sinuous tail, as pink as a baby's eyelids.
Up in the tower, Ratpunzel squeaked and
chittered with glee – how all that climbing
tickled her vertebrae. She preened
her whiskers in the mirror and applied
ruby-red lipstick to her flabby muzzle.
"Ah Ratpunzel, why do I love you so?"
cried the royal climber as he clambered
through the window. The she-rat
fluttered her greasy lashes as she squealed,
"Because I'm a rat-witch, I've cast my spell
and you shall never be free. For who
knows traps better than a rat?"
But the Prince wasn't listening.
Men in love hear only three things:
their own witty remarks, the word 'Yes'
and bedsprings. From his belt hung
a sack and this he opened, revealing
wax-coated lumps of cheese shaped
like hearts. "Are they Gouda 'nuf
for you?" he jested. "Are you going to
Edam all up?"

How quickly love turns to utter
disgust. With a sneer, the rat-witch
snatched up the laughing Prince
and flung him headfirst
straight out the window.

29.

Horror House of Thumb

See that tiny baby-blue house
in the shadow of the catalpa tree?
It's the one next to that dead oak
filled with spiderwebs.
That insidious little house of horrors –
that's where Tom Thumb used to live.
That's where he took his victims.
Being so small drove him mad –
as mad as a weensy hatter
sucking on an itsy-bitsy crack-pipe.
They say he tortured an
entire family of butterflies
in there – even the larvae!
Those poor, innocent caterpillars!
Folks say their pitiful screams
could be heard
from four inches away.

But Tom Thumb didn't stop there.
That unholy micro-sadist
pulled the legs off grasshoppers
and used them to build
the framework of his ghastly bed!
For a mattress, he stole
a baby's left sock and stuffed it
with the springy corpses
of all those dead caterpillars.

A monster, that's what he was!
Right up until last week, when
he went to a big-people party
and drank a whole spoonful
of dark beer. He fell asleep
in an ashtray and was killed
when somebody put out a cigar
on his face.

30.

Saved from a Grizzly Demise

His name was Gordon Lockes
and his crazy, sleepless life
as a Channel 19 Action News reporter
was giving him an ulcer and
irritable bowel syndrome, so
he decided to take a week off.
Out in the country. Far, far away
from cameras, shotguns, sirens,
morgues and toe-tags.
He bought some camping supplies
and drove out of the city,
past the pretty lawns of the suburbs,
into the country, into the woods.
Without a map. He wanted to
get lost. And that's one thing
you can always get for free.

He turned left at the dead tree
filled with webs. Spiders are wise,
timeless, magical creatures –
practically eight-legged sorcerers.
Yeah, those quiet types, they're
the tricky ones.

Gordon drove up to a cabin –
actually, more of a cottage,
since it had a thatched roof.
Quaint. Touristy. Maybe it was
a bed & breakfast. He knocked at
the front door and it swung
inward. In fact, it had been hinged
to swing both ways. Strange.
And why was the door so wide,
with no handles or locks?
Did the owner just barge
in and out, like some kind

of wild animal?

Inside, he smelled something
yummy. On the table were three bowls
of what looked like cooked cereal.
Big bowl, little bowl,
medium-sized bowl in-between.
By the hearth, he saw three chairs.
Big chair, little chair,
medium-sized chair in-between.
At the other end of the cottage,
three beds. Big bed, little bed,
you get the picture.

He turned around at the sound
of a low growl. He found
himself facing a wall of
fur, fangs, claws, death.
"The things you see when
your gun's in the truck,"
he moaned.
Mama and Papa Bear
ripped off Gordon's shirt
so it wouldn't get caught
in their teeth. Then Baby Bear
saw Gordon's stocky, hairy chest.
And Baby – who wasn't a baby
any more, since she'd reached
maturity that summer – said,
"Hold on a second. Is that
any way to treat a guest?
Maybe the nice man
would like some porridge...?"

That night, while
Gordon and Baby Bear chatted
under the stars, Mama Bear
lumbered off to the tower
of the witch Ratpunzel
to borrow a bucket of

transformation body-splash.
Baby birds must leave the nest
sometime, and the same
applies to baby bears. Later,
Mama doused her darling daughter
as Papa roared to the new couple,
"I now pronounce you
man and wife!" In the forest,
bears are allowed to perform
weddings. Actually, they're allowed
to do whatever they want.
Gordon gave his lovely young bride
a kiss, and in the morning, Bibi –
as good a human name as any –
put on some of Gordon's things
and the happy couple drove back
into the city. Mama and Papa Bear
now have extra room to stretch out
while they're hibernating, and
Gordon and Bibi are the proud parents
of a rough-and-ready, burly lad
who is doing extremely well
in the Cub Scouts.

31.

Wicked Queen

She was born
with a black umbilical cord.
She has blood-red lips, purple eyelids
and lustrously long, thick black lashes –
and that's without her make-up.
Her scarlet nails naturally grow into
needle-thin points. Her insidious gaze
makes any mirror magical.
Glass paperweights become mystic
crystal balls when stroked gently,
lovingly by her claws. She is a creature
of beautiful horror and horrible beauty,
as cold and delicate as ice crystals
in a winter spiderweb. She is exquisite,
unique – and without companion.
Nature does not dare to create
her mate, and no lesser creature
has the courage to woo her.

Shadows long and monsters tall,
who is the saddest one of all?
The answer can be found
in her mirror.

32.

Ashley

Through Ashley's childhood,
all the other kids teased him –
"Ashley's a girl's name,
so Ashley must really be a girl,
'cuz he likes having a girl's name
so much." The fact that Ashley
was fine-boned and soft-spoken
with long golden hair
didn't help matters. And the
truth was, inside, Ashley felt
like a real girl. A pretty one, too.
But he never let the other kids
know that.

His family was mega-rich
and his parents had lots of time
for business and parties
and shopping and brunches,
but funny, never quite enough
for him. So is it any wonder
he ran away ... or that after
horrid years of loveless liars
and aimless wandering, he
eventually found a dead oak tree
filled with spiderwebs?
That tree, it seems to draw
certain people.

A clump of webs as big as
a man – shaped like one, too –
fell out of the tree. It got up,
shook itself into shape and
stared at Ashley with silver eyes.
"My child," it said, "those rags
will never do. The Wolf
is throwing a ball tonight.

You'll want to look your best."

"A wolf? He'll eat me whole!"
Ashley cried. "I'm looking
for a prince."

The man with silver eyes
shrugged. "Wolf. Prince.
You think too much. It's just
a dance." He waved to the spiders
and they all swirled down and
around Ashley, spinning up
a shining silken gown, soft yet
strong, perfect for an evening of
waltzes and meaningful glances.

That night, the guests
oohed and aahed as Ashley
swirled across the ballroom floor
in the arms of the Wolf, who
wore a soldier's uniform.
It seemed appropriate, since his
was a life of constant strife.
"You dance like an angel,"
the carnivore declared.
"I would hate for you to
flutter away. My heart would
shatter like a glass slipper
flung into the fireplace."

"So you say," Ashley purred.
"but just look at your outfit.
You're dressed like a brute,
a killer. Am I to believe
a wolf in creep's clothing?
Your lips form words of love,
but they can't hide those
big teeth of yours. I want
Prince Charming, not one
so alarming."

"How you misconstrue!" replied
the Wolf. "Who mentioned
love? I only wish to dance
and chat. To spend some time,
no more, no less. Stay a few days.
Your prince will wait,
wherever he is."

Midnight came and went,
and still they danced. And Ashley
stayed. Days turned into weeks
and every night, they danced
and laughed and talked about
all sorts of things, like the life
of a wolf, or a boy who thinks
he's a girl. The weeks turned into
months ... months into years
and years and years ... until one day,
while walking through the woods,
the man with silver eyes saw
a gray-haired, slender someone,
kneeling by a grave. And the man
asked, "How was the dance? I see
he didn't eat you."

Ashley's tears fell like rain
upon thirsty ground. "I wish
he had. We'd still be together
that way."

What have we learned?
Maybe nothing. Maybe this:
In a world of uncertainty,
hardship and lies,
a boy can still weep
when a faithful dog dies.

33.

Joe White

Oh, it was terrible
the day Joe White marched
down the road, past the dead tree
clotted with spiderwebs,
took the turn near the swamp,
went another half-mile until
he saw seven little mailboxes
all in a row, and stomped
right up to the door of
the baby-blue-edged-with-pink
cottage of the half-dozen-plus-one
diminutive gentlemen.
"Come on out, you slimy
half-pint degenerates!
Shack up with my daughter,
will you? Now you're gonna
get a taste of grade-A
homogenized whoop-ass!"

Unfortunately, Snow's seven
height-challenged suitors were
not especially bright. They thought
whoop-ass sounded like some kind
of fancy dessert, so they all came
tumbling merrily out of the
pretty cottage. They looked so
eager, too, like Christmas urchins
expecting presents.

A bullet is a present
that commits its recipient
to the past tense.
The gun was a six-shooter,
so Joe clubbed the last one
until his wee skull cracked.
The poor thing didn't die.
After that, he was just
dopey.

34.

Loved Her, Hated Him

"Me and the missus," said a friend
of mine other day, "we were at
their house last night. You know the ones.
That gorgeous, blue-eyed hotty
and that sickening creature
she calls hubby. What the Hell
is he supposed to be, anyway?
He has a hog's wet, hairy snout,
the eyes of a giant grasshopper,
a forked tongue, beagle ears,
and a body like a giant slug.
He brays like a crazy donkey
and spits when he talks.
They live in a run-down castle
in the deep, dark woods –
head down the road, turn left
at the dead tree filled with
spiderwebs, then turn right,
then left, then right again.
Three miles later, you're there.
Not that anybody with half a brain
would want to go there."

My friend paused to suck down
some of his gin and tonic. "As for
me and the missus," he continued,
"we had to go. It was the hotty's
birthday, and my wife is her
sister. I do love my wife, but
man oh man, that hotty is a real
knock-out beauty – how she ever
got mixed up with a goofy beast
like her hubby, I'll never know.
Why, he doesn't even have
antlers or poisonous quills,
like me."

35.

Kiss

Blue-eyed, square-jawed
young Percival wished
to awaken the fair maiden
with a kiss. A Wicked Queen
had cast a slumber-spell
on the pretty miss ages ago,
and only a juicy lip-lock
from Mr. Right would
pop her out of that coma.

Alas, sleep was, is and
always shall be
an enemy of fresh breath.
The sweet maiden's
dainty pink tongue was now
coated with yellow fur, and
stank like a truck-stop toilet
filled with fermented guano
and Limburger cheese
three months after its
expiration date.

Just as Percival's lips
approached hers,
she happened to exhale.
Her breath poached his eyeballs
and turned the skin of his face
into sand.

36.

Stalked

Jack's mommy said, "I'm sick
of that stinking cow. Five drops
of milk, that's all I could squeeze
out of her this morning. Sell her
in the village. Maybe the butcher
can chop her into catfood." So
scrawny, gaptoothed, fatherless
Jack tied some twine around
the cow's neck and led it down
the road. By a dead oak tree
filled with spiderwebs, he met
a man with silver eyes.
"Give me the cow and you
shall never be alone," the man said.
"Look. I have something
just for you." Into Jack's hand
he dropped a blue seed, shaped
like a baby girl.

Jack's mommy beat him
that night and threw the seed
out the window. "No brains,
just like your stupid dead father,"
she said. "No supper for you!"
Jack cried on his pile of straw
in his cold little room for hours.
Then he felt something stroke
his jaw – a slender hand with
long blue leaves for fingers.
The hand was attached to a
sinuous, leafy arm reaching
in through his window.
The hand was gentle, but Jack
was not used to such kindness.
"Help me!" he cried, rushing out
of his room and into mommy's.

There, another blue hand, reaching
in through another window,
had just finished strangling
the woman to death. Jack ran
out of the cottage, right into
a writhing, growing flurry
of blue-leaved hands and stalks
that wouldn't let him go. Oh no.
They carried him skyward to
a jungle hidden in the clouds,
then pulled their roots up
behind them – a clean escape
from Earth. Caring hands pressed
chunks of juicy blue fruit
into his mouth. "Eat," rustled
the leaves. "Grow. Eat. Grow into
my giant." So little Jack ate and ate
until he was quite blue in the face.
His belly swelled and swelled just
like a balloon, until suddenly,
vines began popping out of his
armpits, nipples, navel and some
other funny spots. He's still
up there, you know. With that
lady stalk, way up high in the
cloud-jungle. Growing in the sun.
Now and then, they drop their
roots down, down, down into
some thick, black river mud.
Dinner for two.

Now look
into my silver eyes
and tell me:
Are you lonely?
Are you?
I thought so.
Hold out your hand.
I have something
just for you.

MOTHER GOOSE, COOKED TO PERFECTION
by Michael McCarty

37.

Zombie Jack Spratt

Zombie Jack Spratt
Would eat no fat
His zombie wife ate no lean
Yet when they dined
On human flesh
They licked the platter clean

38.

Jack Be Dinner

Jack be nimble
Jack be quick
Jack be tasty
When served with dip

39.

Old Mother Hubbard's Kennel of Blood

Old Mother Hubbard
Went to her cupboard
To fetch her poor dog a bone
When she got there
The cupboard was bare
So the dog attacked the crone

COSMIC HORRORS, UNIVERSAL PICTURES:
MYTHOS MONSTERS STAR IN CLASSIC HORROR FILMS
by Mark McLaughlin

40.

Nyarlathenstein

I wanted to create – from death! –
a creature that would walk the Earth
in a pleasing form. And so I did.
Piece by piece, I stitched dead flesh
into a crazy quilt of beauty.
Lightning – cosmic power! –
energized the lovely mess and soon,
my demon-angel shuddered
and drew breath. It's alive! It's alive!
Wild beasts now lovingly lick
the seams of its hands
and street-wretches grovel
at its mismatched feet.
It has become a scientist,
just like me, and even as I speak,
it is building a machine
to bring dead gods to life.

41.

Cthulhu's Daughter

But don't you see? I want to be
a normal, happy woman,
one who laughs, dances, sings,
and plays jolly songs on the piano.
But my father–! Never shall I
escape his ancient curse.
The cold black brine that is his blood
courses through my veins.
My soul swims ever downward
into baleful ocean trenches. I long
for endlessly swirling currents,
the slick caress of webbed fingers
and writhing tentacles.
I shall be going out this evening
and at dawn, another body
will be found by the river
with livid sucker marks
upon the throat.

42.

Pickman's Werewolf

My dear old chum was a painter
of strange tableaus, and gallery patrons
would eek and squeak and shriek
at his gruesome scenarios.
"How in the world, Pickman,
do you conjure up such images
of fur and fangs?" I queried.
"Your nightmare paintings feature
upright creatures – and the very sight
of five hairy, outstretched claws
does give me pause." His answer?
"Come to my studio tonight,
my friend, while the Autumn moon
is full and bright." So I did – and never
shall I forget how a howling thing
from Hell's foul pits tore my friend
to bits, and chased me round
and round. I knocked an easel down
and later, in my hand I found
a crumpled photo, snatched up
in my haste. Satan's camera snapped
that ghastly shot, in which
a lanky canine horror stooped to nuzzle
something bloated, white and puffy
with its muzzle

43.

The Colour from the Blasted Lagoon

Shining chunks of living metal
from beyond space and time
plummeted into the rainforest lagoon
and for a wild hour, bubbles
of a most peculiar Colour
roiled and boiled and seethed.
The jungle trees, vines and flowers
grew with lurid, lavish opulence
in the season that followed.
Succulent orchids, as big as pigs
and glowing with the Colour,
whipped the air with plump,
leafy tentacles. Batwinged moths
and three-eyed, long-haired bees
hopped hungrily from blossom
to poisonous blossom,
sucking down mad nectar.
But soon, the fish, turtles, lizards
and frogs warped and shriveled
into twisted parodies of themselves.
The gorgeous, engorged flowers
rotted into thick, gray piles of grit
and the flying things hit the dirt.
Still, not everything died:
the lagoon's most peculiar denizen –
the Creature – actually thrived
and grew more peculiar still.
Scaly green hide turned slick
and pink. The gills slapped shut
as heaving lungs bloomed within.
The Creature emerged from the lagoon
as a man, and even now he is heading
toward bright city lights,
his eyes glowing with a Colour
never before designated
on any driver's license.

SLIMY CREATURES FROM OUTER SPACE
by Michael McCarty

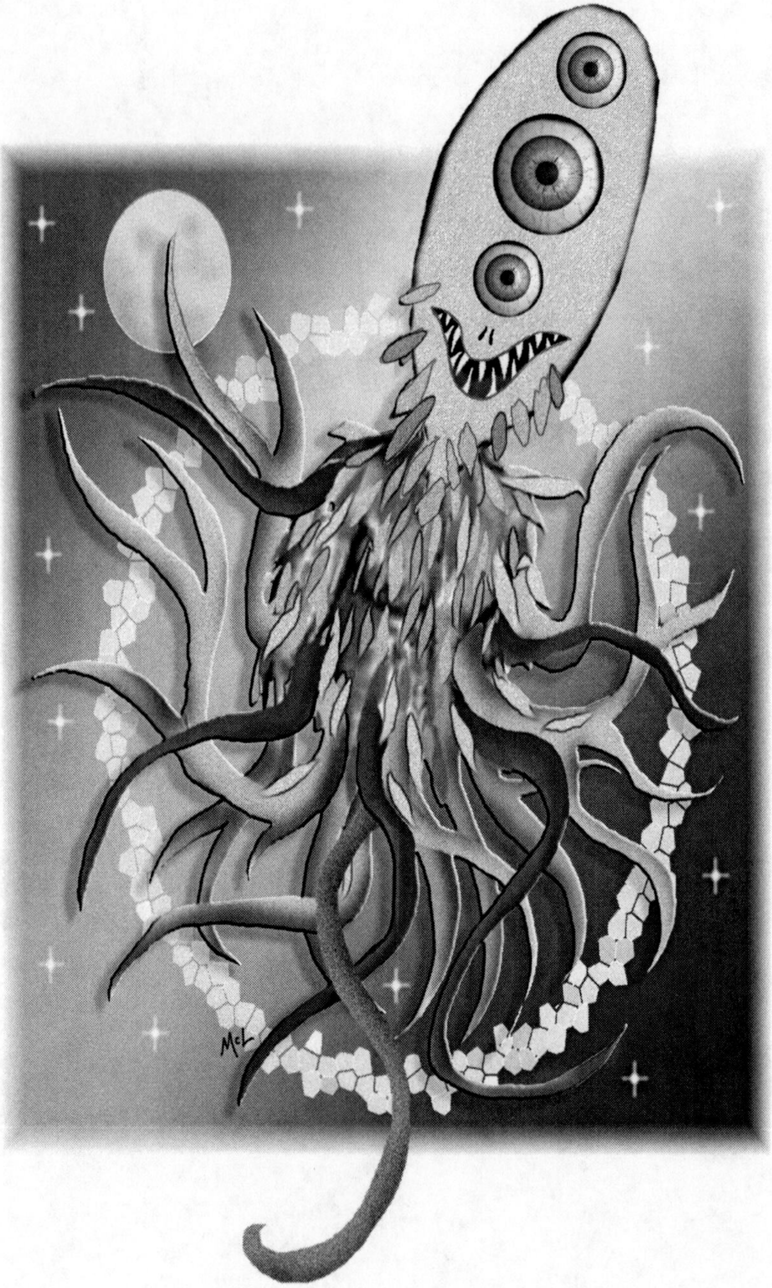

INTRODUCTION:

My name is Agent Michael McCarty and I work for the Federal Report on Extraterrestrial Aliens And Knitting Seniors – FREAKS for short. Under a different name, FREAKS used to document UFO activities exclusively, but with recent budget cuts, our department had to be combined with research on the knitting habits of senior citizens. Believe me, there are a lot of seniors knitting out there.

The Freedom Of Information Act mandates that we must disclose our activities to the general public. Submitted for your edification is a collection of noteworthy alien case studies. Because of the budget cuts, we composed these studies in verse, to attain additional literary grant funding. Even with that, we'll probably still have to hold a few bake sales.

Aliens. Fact? Fiction? You be the judge.

Michael McCarty
Senior FREAKS Agent

44.

Document: 669-996
Topic: Escaped ET
Alien Prisoner
(with Agent Sandy DeLuca)

Time and space
space and time
blend together
in the alien's eyes

The creature
from another planet
found he could
bend time backwards
when his starship
spun in reverse

Sheds bell-bottoms,
flowered shirt,
love beads bought
in a shed while
cruising through the '60s
during the Mardi Gras –
nobody noticed
his bug-eyes and
lime-green complexion.

Safe in the vacuum
of time, he carefully
checks dials,
measures movement
of planets,
calculates the when
and where of the next eclipse
spinning around and around

Back and forth
through eternity,

swinging to big band
beats in the forties,
a minuet during the
French Revolution,
Rave was big in
the twenty-first century

So much for the parties,
the meaningless sex,
millennium –
moonlit adventures

The creature was
en route to the
prison planet
killed the crew
and stole the ship
to Earth
he had so much fun
on the third blue planet
circling all so fast

The ship cruised Greece
and he stalked Helen of Troy
her face could launch
a thousand ships
but between her legs
could launch even more

Went to Rome
and saw Nero play his lyre
as the great city burned
tripped the emperor
and he burned too

He coiled Cleopatra's serpent
around his neck
then spun off to the Wild West
and planted the writhing reptile
inside Annie Oakley's hat

Stole the greatest art treasurers
ravished history's beautiful women
drank fine wine throughout time
money – all so much money

All along
his starship
spinning fast and faster
around the universe like a top

But like Icarus
the ship flew too close to the Sun
a welcome execution after all

45.

Document: 000000000000000-0
Topic: Cereology
Crop Circles

All the farms in Hicksville, Iowa
had crop circles.
you know –
those circular, swirled-flat
cut-outs in the middle of
wheat, barley and corn fields.

Every single farm except for
Hank Atkin's place.
He'd brag down at the barber shop,
"No crop circles here!"
he'd say, as Old Joe
gave him a trim.
"And if some
little green man
ever steps on my land
I'll blast him back
to the stars."
The town folk started
gossiping about why Hank
had no crop circles.
Wasn't it strange,
during last year's drought
when most folks
couldn't even grow weeds,
Atkin's farm was flourishing?
And wasn't it weird,
a few years before,
when it rained and rained
and washed away most crops,
Hank's corn stood tall?
Wasn't that peculiar?

Sheriff Arlo Barnes

decided to investigate.
Late one night,
the lawman drove over
to Hank's place –
and parked
out front of the pig pen
was a big-ass spaceship.

The Sheriff drew out his
flashlight and six-shooter,
slowly crept around
to the side of the house
and peered into
the dark windows, looking
for some kind of answer.

In Hank's bedroom,
the officer found
the startling truth.

Right there
in the farmer's bed,
Hank was snuggling
a little green lady
from outer space.

"No crop circles here!"
Hank yelled to the sheriff
as the intergalactic couple
cuddled under the covers.

46.

Document: 2cute
Topic: Adorable Aliens
Cute, Cuddly Creatures from Another Planet

They looked like little pink teddy bears,
those cute, cuddly creatures from another planet.
Ready for destruction, armed to the teeth,
They planned on taking over the Earth.

They landed in their little flying saucers
at a playground in L.A.
Kids by the dozens swarmed them,
saying "Oh mommy, aren't they so cute!"
and kissing them and hugging them.

This ticked off the aliens
and they cooed angrily,
but the coos got woos from the kids.
"They are so adorable!" one little tyke
said with a precious smile.

The cute, cuddly creatures
barely made it back to their spaceships
They were almost loved to death.
Defeated, they flew back to their planet.

47.

Document: 90210
Topic: Alien Actor
Gone Hollywood

IT! was the best damn actor
from the planet with three suns,
watching old sci-fi movies via satellite.
IT! studied how the Earth stood still,
why it came from outer space,
learned it's best not to marry a monster from another planet.

IT! could mimic every move Gort made.
The creature could even do all those dorky hand signals
from the grand finale of Close Encounters.
IT! even ate Reese's Pieces like E.T.

IT! took a flying saucer to Earth,
Hollywood to be exact.
IT! went from studio to studio to studio,
audition after audition after audition,
and was told it couldn't act.

Hollywood just wasn't ready
for a seventeen-foot spider to play
a monster from outer space

48.

Document: RUNUTS2
Topic: Trust No One
Not One of Us

I know THEY are watching me,
every day from dusk till dawn.
THEY want to kill me and
bury me under my lawn.

In the darkness THEY whisper,
"You're not one of us" –
Am I going crazy?
There's no one I can trust.

THEY eat away my brain.
My mind is not the same.
I put a gun inside my mouth
To end this cruel game.

49.

Document: OU812
Topic: Immigration
Illegal Aliens

illegal aliens work cheap
all you have to do
is feed them raw meat
whenever managers
shout and get cross
illegal aliens
will eat their boss

50.

Document: 123-8954
Topic: Roswell Revealed
Area 51, Where Are You?

Where is this Area 51
that all the conspirators
talk about?
I heard it is in
Roswell, Arizona,
Wherever the hell
that is.
Long time ago
Senator Goldwater,
that bloated blowhard,
cussed like a sailor
when asked about it.
Potty-mouth senator,
Is Area 51 a storage bin
for dead Martians?
Or is it a secret
country club
for all the glamorous,
planet-hopping
nouveau riche aliens?

51.

Document: 4441
Topic: Robert Silverberg's NYC
The Others
(with Agent Sandy DeLuca)

Abandoned subway stations
in New York;
refuge for the homeless,
shelter for rodents and bats;
wormholes of space and time

The city grows,
makes love, and breeds
around and above;
Never seeing silver spaceships
and slithery beings crawl through

The Sun disappears;
a harsh cold wind blows,
as people huddle for warmth –
and The Others walk the streets
The Others drag
yet another child aboard;
people try to ignore
the screams and cries for help;
there is no place to hide and
any one of them could be next

52.

Document: bigbooty1
Topic: Da Butt
Alien Anal Probe

I always thought it was kinda weird
that creatures from across the universe
would come all the way to Earth
just to probe someone's ass.

I mean, wouldn't the aliens be more interested
in our science, our history – our TV shows?
Why would they just want to stick
something up our butts?

Whatever their motive, I only hope
if they ever come to Earth
to probe me, I'll at least get
dinner and a movie first.

53.

Document: 25225
Topic: Fashion Impaired
MIB

The men in black
wear black hats
black shades
black clothes
and drive black Cadillacs

When the MIB talk,
they sound like
Joe Friday from Dragnet.
"Here's the facts, Ma'am.
There's no such things
As UFOs.
And don't sell your story
to the tabloids.
If you do,
we'll steal your cat."

Forget about Will Smith
or Tommy Lee Jones
from the movies,
or even Alex Trebek
and Jesse Ventura
from The X-Files.
Did you ever wonder about
Johnny Cash –
He wore all black.
Did you ever notice
He didn't blink when he sang?

54.

Document 26226
Topic: Sci-Fi Sequels
MIB II

Johnny Cash died
before MIB II was released
maybe he didn't want to
sit through the lame sequel

Did we really need Part Two?
Like there were so many
unanswered questions:
"Where's Mr. Smith going to spend
all those millions?" and
"Can they possibly milk the cash-cow even more
for MIB III?"

55.

Document: 90210-B
Topic: More Sequels
War of the Worlds

H.G. Wells once wrote a novel
Called War of the Worlds
Orson Welles –
No relation to H.G. –
turned it into a radio show
that caused panic on the airwaves

Then in Hollywood, 1953,
director Byron Haskin
screenwriter Barry Lyndon
and star Gene Barry
turned it into a blockbuster movie

In the '70s there was
that rock 'n' roll album
with Justin Hayward from The Moody Blues
and David Essex
Martians rocking out as they invaded earth

And let's not even talk about
that lame TV series War of the Worlds
that ran about two seasons
from 1988 to 1990

In 2005, almost 52 years later,
Hollywood remade War of the Worlds
with superstar Tom Cruise
and superdirector Stephen Spielberg

Too bad
none of the above
read the book

56.

Document: bigbooty2
Topic: More Of Da Butt
It Came from Uranus

Uranians,
the sludgy brown creatures
from Uranus,
stink to high heaven
and leave skid marks
when they walk.

Only two people
could stand their stench –
an old man who'd lost his
sense of smell and
a street-person who
lived in a sewer.
When they asked the aliens,
"Where did you come from?"
and they replied,
"Uranus!"
even those two ran off.
The Uranians
really don't mind.
They're used to being alone.
Uranus
is a lonely place.

57.

Document: FOX18
Topic: Autopsies on Aliens
Alien Autopsy

I didn't bother watching
Alien Autopsy to the end.
What a rinky-dinky production,
taped on cheap video
with a jerky camera!
It jumps around more
than that Blair Witch flick.

I laughed when they cut open
that poor little green man
and pulled out six feet of goop
that looked more like Silly String
than any alien's intestines.

I guess that's the kind of
scholarly entertainment
you can expect from tabloid TV.
As popular as it was, I wonder
if there's a sequel in the works –
Alien Funeral?

58.

Document: 413498890998881111118
Topic: Unmarked Helicopter
Lights from the Sky

I stood on my back porch
just looking at the stars
when all of a sudden
I saw some lights
coming right out of the sky

Now I've read enough tabloids
to know about UFOs,
and since I live out here in
the country, no one for miles,
I'd welcome any alien folk.

This man all in green
came running up to my porch
saying something about his
secret chopper crashing.
He spoke good English.

Then suddenly more lights
came from the sky
and there were tanks,
jeeps, all kinds of
military vehicles.

Some fancy general
with a bunch of medals
said I knew too much.
Now I'm stuck in
this military installation
for God knows how long.

That's what I get
for looking at the stars.

59.

Document: 387-YUCK
Topic: Only the Lonely
The Slimy Monster from Outer Space

the slimy monster from outer space
was seven feet tall
with an ugly face
one eyeball
and of course
all that slime

the slimy monster from outer space
could fly
a spaceship
across the
universe
in reverse

the slimy monster from outer space
had no relatives
no friends
no buddies
no sidekicks
zero dates

yes the slimy monster from outer space
was a lonely creature
with an ugly face
but inside that
slimy chest
beats a sad blue heart

SPEAKING PARTS: FRANKENSTEIN'S MONSTER RESTITCHED AS A BODY OF VERSE
by Mark McLaughlin

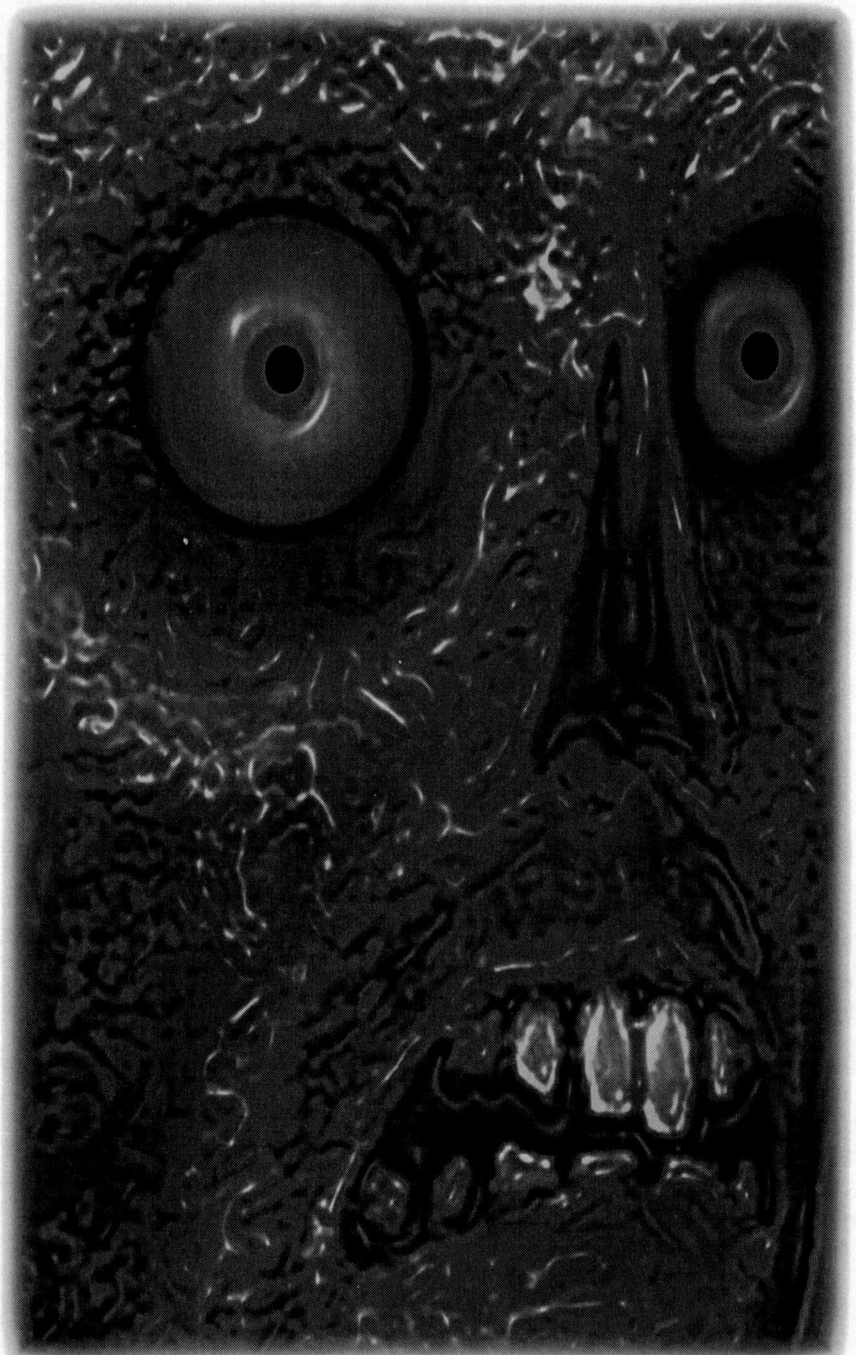

60.

I Am the Monster's Navel

Why did Dr. Frankenstein even
stitch me onto this mess?
Just for show, I suppose.
The Monster was never born –
waking up a pile of dead flesh
isn't birth. The only cord attached
to him while he was on the slab
was electrical – a crazy-ass jumper cable.
I used to belong to a weightlifter
with a golden tan and perfect abs,
who didn't mind showing off.
Now I'm just a grubby little hole,
a receptacle for the filth
that dribbles down from
the Monster's gnawing mouth,
the bits of gore that slide down
his neck, his chest, his bloated belly,
into me.

61.

I Am the Monster's Penis

I was cut
from the corpse of a short guy
with a dreary office job
and a big mouth.
"Hey, honey! If I told you
you had a nice body, would you
hold it against me?" Lines older
than Mae West's girdle.
Always trying to sweet-talk secretaries
into bed, so he could
put me to work.
Such a fuss.
As far as the Monster's concerned,
I'm just a spout for his dark,
stinking piss,
handy for drowning
ant colonies.

62.

I Am the Monster's Heart

My original owner
was a guy who kept changing jobs:
one day a clerk at a health food store,
the next a waiter – or a truck driver,
janitor, musician (he played the guitar
quite well, actually). His girlfriend,
a dental hygienist, made good money
so when the baby came, he didn't see
any reason for him to pay
for any aspect of its existence.
Yeah, he called the kid 'it.'
What a guy.
The mother eventually moved away
and didn't bother sending him
a postcard with her new address.
No check were forthcoming,
so why waste a stamp?

Now I pulse
for yet another
cold, aimless beast.

63.

I Am the Monster's Fifth Kidney

It's a hell of a job,
trying to filter the toxins out of
this freaky bastard's system.
There's nothing he won't stuff
into that chomping mouth of his.
And when he gets thirsty,
there's no fluid too vile or chunky
for him. He'll swill it down
without a second thought,
assuming that he indeed thinks.
I think that's why the doctor
put five of us in here.
Even with all that assistance,
I've got my work cut out for me.

I used to belong to a priest.
He drank a lot, but he usually
fell asleep after four or five drinks,
so I always had enough time
to clean house. Plus,
he didn't eat as much meat
as the Monster. Last night,
the damned thing ate two babies,
part of a dog, and an old woman's
brain. Most of her face, too.
Doesn't that stupid creature realize
that too much protein
is bad for me?

64.

I Am the Monster's Right Knee

I knelt
in front of
a lot of men.
I was a man.
And there was nothing wrong
with any of that. I'm not sorry.
It was what I did.
But I doubt if
I'll ever get to do that again.
No one's about to ask.
Besides, the Monster
is more of a
biter.

65.

I Am the Monster's Left Ear

Blah
blah blah
blah blah blah
blah blah blah blah –
You get the idea.
That's why my previous owner
killed her husband. My delicate,
daintily lobed splendor
could only take so much.
A fine-boned hand picked up a knife
and did a little stabbing.
To silence the blabbing.
So look where I am now.
Sewn onto this raw, ugly,
hideous man-thing,
constantly listening
to his idiot roar.

66.

I Am the Monster's Bottom Lip

I used to sing,
used to wrap myself
around such delightful sentiments.
I used to kiss – oh, how soft I was,
once upon a time.
I'm still soft. With decay.
A little tattered, too.
The Monster keeps ripping me
by accident. I suppose someday
he'll bite me clean off.
But then,
that would probably be
for the best.

67.

I Am the Monster's Pinky

I'm the only one here
who has it better now.
Previously, I belonged
to a bank president
who used to pick his nose
with me. All the time.
Even in meetings.
The other bank executives
would all just look at
their notes, the walls,
whatever.
Fortunately, the Monster's
desiccated nasal tissues
don't produce snot,
so at least I have been spared
that.

68.

I Am the Monster's Stomach

I used to belong to a fat English woman
who had a cooking show on public TV.
I used to dine on exquisite roast pheasant,
stuffed with brandied raisins and plums –
that was my favorite, back then.
And now? Our latest meal
was a wine-addled old bum
he'd cornered in an alley.
Oh dear. Not quite roast pheasant.
At least the Monster keeps me full
and is constantly surprising me.
It's amazing what one
gets used to, in time.
I suppose I should be thankful
that I'm not in a grave,
serving as a banquet
for worms.

69.

I Am the Monster's Hazel Eye

The Monster has a blue left eye
and a hazel right one. Me.
I once belonged to a cocktail waitress
named Barbara. A single mother.
For a while she'd been an exotic dancer,
but she'd changed jobs during the pregnancy.
She named the baby Duane, after
her third-grade teacher, a nice old guy
who'd once given her a B+.
She sure as Hell wasn't going to
name her kid after the dad –
an abusive loser, a used car salesman with
a drinking problem – or her own dad,
another boozer. He used to slap her around
and do worse than that
whenever he felt the need for a little
companionship.

Monsters. They're a dime a dozen.

70.

I Am the Monster's Thumb

The doctor cut me off
a hitch-hiker he'd picked up
late one night. The young man
didn't fight it. How could he?
The doctor had caved in his head
with a sledgehammer.
I'd always enjoyed pointing
down the road, because that's
where one eventually found
money, love, the future.
Down the road.
But I have a feeling
the road I'm on now
doesn't lead to a glorious sunset.
No, it only leads into a cold, starless
night without end.
It's a sad, pitiful road.
But at least it's a road.

71.

I Am the Monster's Sphincter

I was a swirly-sliced out of the cadaver
of a writer-cum-literary-critic
with a rage disorder.
He loved classic literature
but could not churn out any
himself. So he hated everyone
and gave other writers
bad reviews. He loved to
make people feel stupid with his
smirking, caustic comments.
Eventually he took
his own life.

The Monster has a big appetite,
so I'm put to work
regularly.
Is there any entity
who has ever had to endure
more shit
than me?

72.

I Am the Monster's Brain

There's a little part of me
that remembers some of the fun,
the happiness I used to have.
That's the part telling you
all of this. I used to play Scrabble
and drive a blue car and work in an office.
I had a mug that said WORLD'S BEST –
What? What was I the World's Best at?
I can't remember. But somebody
gave me that mug.
I didn't buy it for myself.
Anyway, there's that little part.
Then there's an ugly, vicious,
horrible part – the big part –
that loves to pound people with rocks
and stick rusty wires in them and
hear them scream for hours on end.
The big part hates me, but then,
it hates itself, too.

It's the hate
that keeps this impossible carcass
moving.

I think the big part is really
everything bad about the me
I used to be. All that bad stuff
had been hidden before.
But after we came back to life
the big part took over.

I can't stand the helplessness.
Having to watch.
Scenes of pain fill me up,
pushing out my old memories
one by one.

World's Best what?
What?

VAMPIRE SEXTETTE
by Michael McCarty

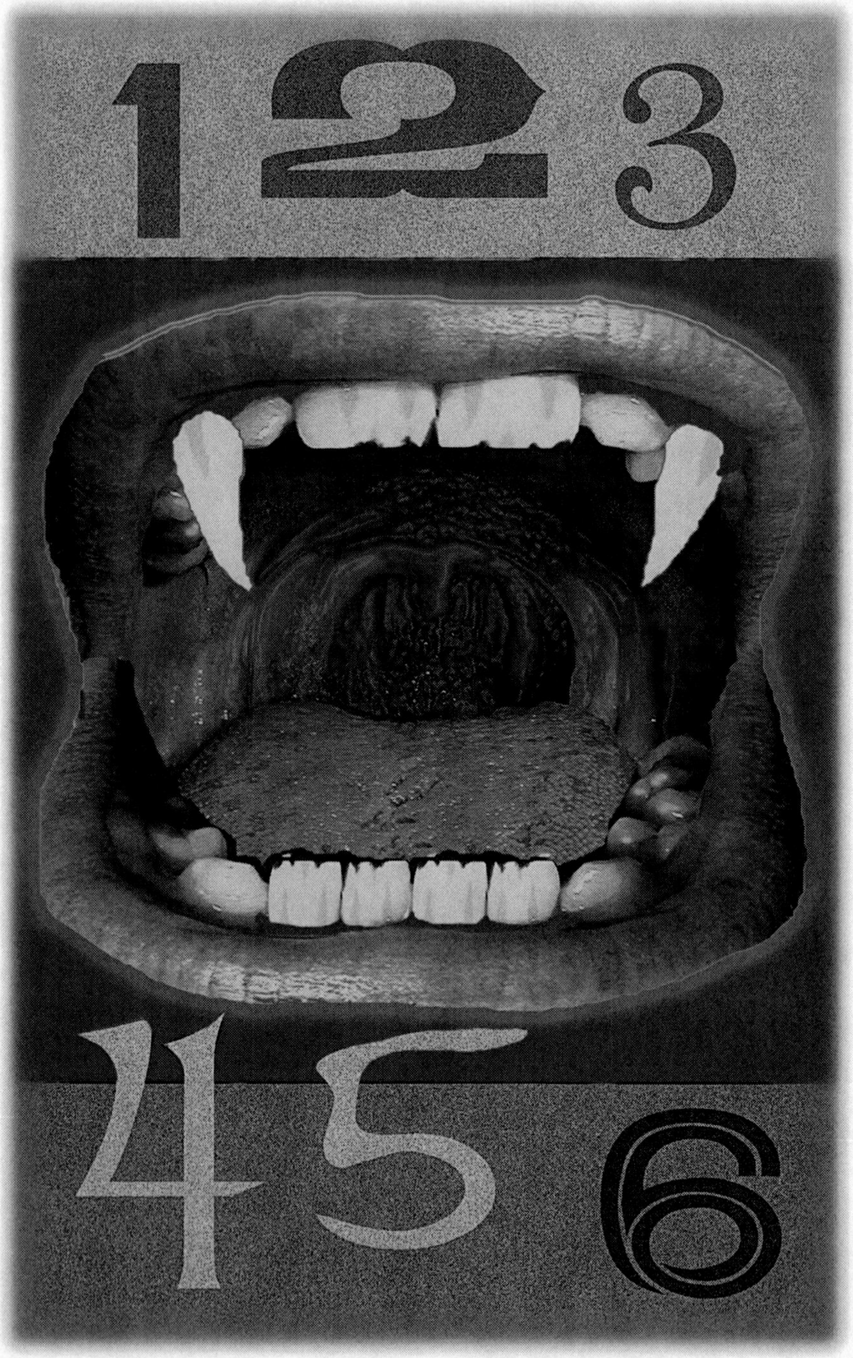
123
456

73.

Beyond the Moonlight
(with Terrie Leigh Relf)

Suffused with orange moonlight,
he waits outside her bedroom window
until she falls asleep, and then
he enters her dreams…
She writhes and moans as
he eases into her bed:
his breath against her ear
his hands linger at her breasts
his tongue explores her nether lips.

He arches his neck to curl around hers
then sinks his razor-sharp fangs into her flesh
She moans with delight
as he bites her again and again
blood drips onto the pillow
her blood flows, pools
He sinks deeper into her
probes her wounds
with warm thick tongue
He bites her again
she awakes
alone in orange moonlight

74.

Succubus

I can't wait to see your dark burning eyes
I can't wait to feel your soft fingertips
I can't wait to hear your echoing voice
Or taste the chill of your sweet bloodless lips

75.

Vampire's Kiss

Who can resist the vampire's kiss?
Temptation and pain swirl like mist.
Who can resist those dark, brooding eyes?
Who can resist those white, silky thighs?
And when the moon is shining bright,
Who can resist the vampire's bite?

76.

Vegas Undead

Wild-eyed showgirls
with skin so white,
passions burning as bright
as the big-city lights.
City of dreams, screams,
money and might,
where day and night
roll together like dice
in an orgy of vice.

77.

Sex with a Vampire

Sex with a vampire
Last all night
You'd better climax
Before dawn's light

Tangled limbs
A bloody mess
Bright red stains
On a white prom dress

Screams of pleasure
Go all the way
Screams of pain
No call the next day

78.

Television

Television
The ultimate vampire
Sucking your life away
One commercial at a time

MONSTER METAL: NECRO-PUNK-ROCK ANTHEM No. 2
by Mark McLaughlin and Michael McCarty

79.

Zombie Insomniacs

Sleep no more! You'd better stay up.
Squealing demons dig their way up –
right into your tacky plastic-covered living room.
No escape, they will defeat you,
scratch and claw and bite and eat you!
Sink into the lava as the Devil seals your doom!

From their graves the corpses creep –
Hell's so loud, they just can't sleep.
Earth shall not recover from the deadly attacks
of those ass-stinking, lava-drinking
Zombie Insomniacs!

Daddy never loved me. Mommy was a whore.
Granny took her teeth out to give blowjobs door-to-door.
Life's just a jumbo-toilet filled with feces and lies!
All you ever think about is cardinal sin.
Death is coming for you with a shit-eating grin.
Your corpse will make a midnight snack for maggots and flies!

From their graves the corpses creep –
Hell's so loud, they just can't sleep
Earth shall not recover from the deadly attacks
of those ass-stinking, lava-drinking
Zombie Insomniacs!

**YOUR HANDY OFFICE GUIDE TO CORPORATE MONSTERS, Part 1:
KISS-UPS, BROWN-NOSERS & OTHER OFFICE ABSURDITIES**
by Mark McLaughlin

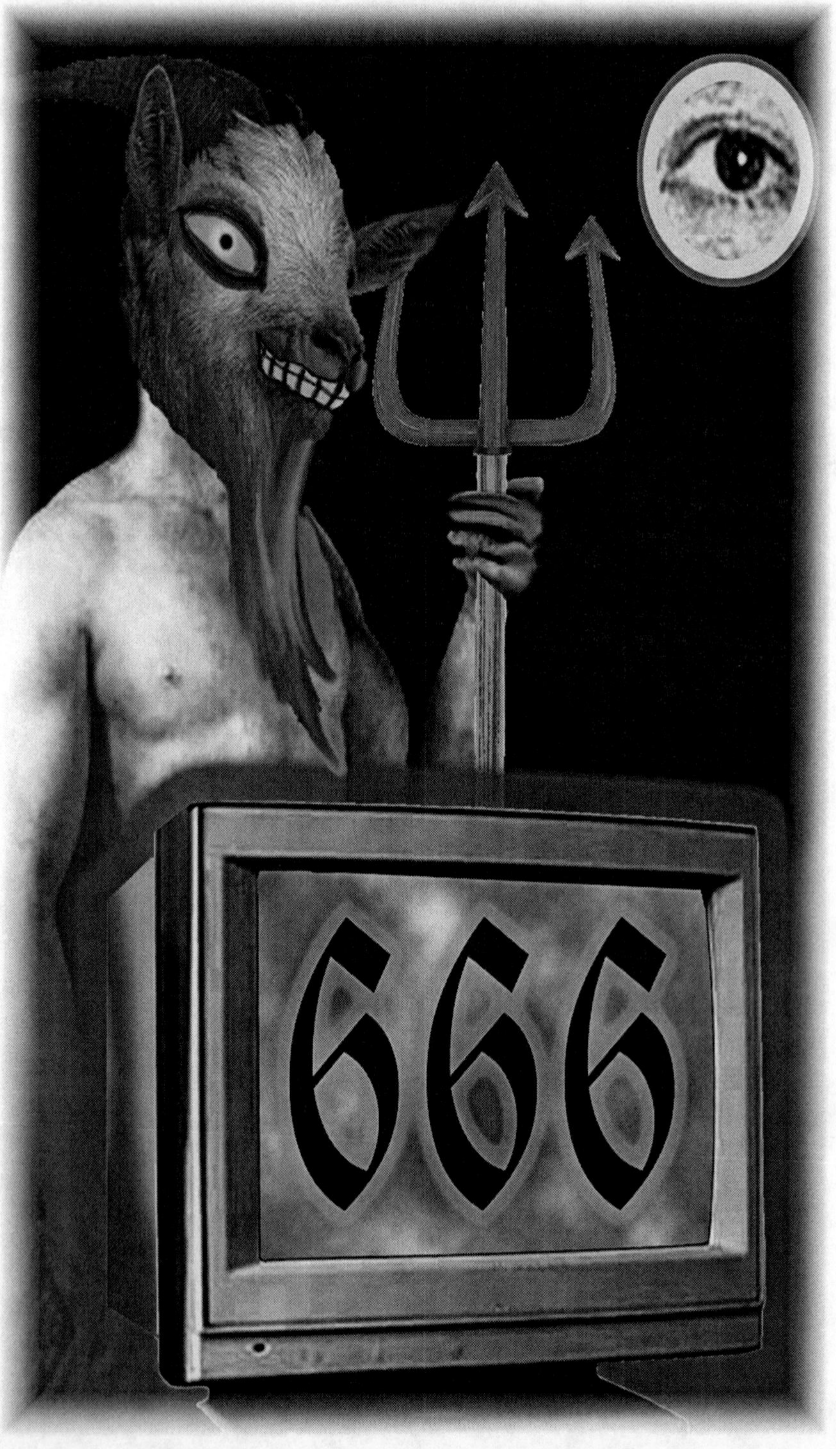
666

80.

The Enthusiraptor

If you have real talent of any sort,
beware the Enthusiraptor!
Enthusiraptors are usually either
Managers or Directors, and if
you have a talent that you enjoy
outside the workplace,
they'll gush all over you and
before you know it, you'll be doing
whatever it is you're good at
for your company. For free.
In addition to your regular duties.
And you won't enjoy it
any more. The Enthusiraptor
is a sort of vampire,
eager to suck the fun
out of your life.

81.

The Fumigorgon

The Fumigorgon is despised by
any being with a functional nose. This
ravenous, health-conscious monster
eats a lot of soy, garlic, seaweed,
fish and cabbage. Teratologists
(folks who study monsters) believe
that Fumigorgons are spawned
when small, stinky yetis breed with
Himalayan mountain-skunks.

The noxious vapors
intermittently emitted by this beast
have been known to induce
nausea, seizures and even madness
in humans. You can always tell
if an office employs a Fumigorgon
who sits near a window. Outside
on the ground below, one will find
a small sad pile
of dead birds and butterflies.

82.

The Normitron

The Normitron is a tightly wound robot
covered with chilly flesh. It just can't stand
anything that's a little … different.
This bland automaton thinks society should
burn comic books (except that nice Richie Rich),
ban horror movies, cancel Halloween,
and pull the plug on those evil video games.
And of course, today's music is just noise!
Male Normitrons wear gray suits
on Casual Fridays. The females only talk
to females of their own kind, because
after all, all other women are either
sluts or lesbians. Normitrons hate
foreign people who have funny accents,
funny clothes and funny religious holidays.
Normitrons often wonder: Why can't those
awful foreign people talk, dress and worship
more like Normitrons?

83.

The Smiling Gladhander

The Smiling Gladhander has a great office
and a big paycheck. It buys people drinks
and pays them loads of compliments
as it boozes and schmoozes its way
to the top. This grinning, oily creature
laughingly calls male colleagues, "You old dog!"
and ask women, "Have you lost weight?"
The Smiling Gladhander has a secretary
who does all its research, handles its calls,
even answers its email. The secretary,
who has to clip coupons to make ends meet,
doesn't have time – or indeed, any reason –
to smile.

84.

The Waffler

The Waffler just can't make up
that clotted clump of spongy tissue
it calls a mind. The Waffler holds meetings
and conducts studies and sends out surveys
to collect and gauge and evaluate
all the opinions of others, so that perhaps
somewhere along the way, after
days and weeks and months spending
tens of thousands of dollars,
it will finally figure out
that the company cafeteria
should stop serving lima beans.

85.

The Spittylicker

For some inexplicable reason,
the Spittylicker can't turn a page
or sort through a stack of papers
without licking its forefinger
or thumb. Maybe it likes the taste
of its own digits. Who knows?
Whenever it has a cold, a dozen
other folks in its department
come down with it, too. Let's hope
that if the Spittylicker ever catches
the ebola virus, it will be
on vacation, far away
at the time.

86.

The Blabberblort

The Blabberblort will tell you all about
who it saw in the grocery store,
what it had for breakfast,
where it will be visiting its mother,
why it needs to go to the doctor,
and in what manner it does or will do
all the above.
Then, just as you open your mouth
to tell a little story of your own,
the Blabberblort will look at its watch
and run off
because for some reason
its behind schedule.

87.

The Potbellied Smirkleflab

The Potbellied Smirkleflab
has the puffy body
of a geriatric pig
and the engorged libido
of a randy teenager.
It will squeeze
a sleazy double-entendre
into the conversation
every chance it gets.
Why? For the same reason
a dog licks itself. Because
it can. Some critters
pride themselves on
their ability to be disgusting.
Don't threaten to drive a stake
into the Potbellied Smirkleflab's
heart. The lusty beast will just
leer at you and say, "Sure,
drive that stake home!
You know you want to!"

88.

The Zitastrophee

The Zitastrophee's apartment
must not have running water,
because it never seems to wash.
The Zitastrophee isn't a teenager,
but it always has two or three,
four or five, six or seven,
maybe even eight or nine or ten
enflamed pimples on its face.
The black horned-rimmed glasses
don't help matters any.
Perhaps one of these days,
the Zitastrophee will learn
of a marvelous space-age substance
known as soap.

The Finicky Foofoo

The Finicky Foofoo is very picky
about the work other do,
and always demands absolute
perfection. It wants its underlings
to show their dedication by
putting in way more than forty
hours a week – and yet,
the Fincky Foofoo's own work
bring new meaning to the term
'mediocre,' and the creature
is always late for meetings,
and leaves work an hour before
everyone else.

Folks paste on their best fake smiles
for the Finicky Foofoo.
But in their hearts, they sincerely wish
it would drop dead.

90.

The Screaming Snotty

The Screaming Snotty always has
a bad word for everyone. It does not
play well with others. People dread
having to deal with it. This minor demon
is damaged goods on two legs – it acts
like a big-shot, but inside, it feels
very small indeed.

Being a Screaming Snotty is both
the crime and its punishment.
Eventually it will give itself
a heart attack and an early grave.
No one will be surprised,
but everyone will be
relieved.

91.

The Caterwauler

The Caterwauler is a subspecies of banshee
that sits in a cubicle, forever staring at a monitor,
loudly calling out for you, always needing
your help. "Duane! Do you have a moment?
Duane! Why is my computer doing this? Duane!
Can you hear me, Duane?" It's not really your job
to fix computers, but the Caterwauler doesn't care.
The Caterwauler just keeps calling your name,
over and over, every time it has a problem.
Why? Because you helped the creature once,
five years ago, and it hasn't forgotten
that kindness.

**YOUR HANDY OFFICE GUIDE TO CORPORATE MONSTERS, Part 2:
CREATURES FROM BEYOND THE CUBICLE**
by Michael McCarty and Mark McLaughlin

92.

The Backstabbing Narkalope

Uh-oh! You went over your lunch hour
by two minutes. That was wrong, so very,
very, VERY wrong – even though you worked
an extra three hours last week. Not that
anyone should care, since you're on salary.
Even so, the Backstabbing Narkalope
WILL report you, and surely, there
WILL be Hell to pay. And perhaps
the Narkalope should make out a
WILL, because one of these days,
someone – maybe you – will bash in
its treacherous little head
with a wrench.

93.

The Sleepy Slothazoid

The Sleepy Slothazoid works
sooo slooooowly, you'd swear
that chilled molasses oozes
through its sluggish veins. Last week,
it took the Slothazoid three hours
to file a marketing report
that was five months old.
And even then, it stuck the report
in the wrong folder
in the wrong filing cabinet
in the wrong building.

94.

The Belligerent Brag-Hag

The Belligerent Brag-Hag takes credit
for everything that everyone else does.
And when I say everything, I mean
EVERYTHING. According to the Brag-Hag,
it wrote, designed, proofed and printed
the annual report, the company newsletter,
and the Encyclopedia Britannica.
It founded the company and erected the building.
It discovered America. It invented fire.
Why, it even created the Earth
while working its way through college
by delivering babies, pizzas and telegrams...
which is truly incredible, when you consider
that the Brag-Hag still lives with
its mother.

95.

The Office Oddball

Hey, did you see that new movie
about the Martian dentist that gives birth
to a two-headed monkey that speaks French?
Of course you didn't. It doesn't exist.
Even so, the Office Oddball will tell you
all about it. That's what oddballs do.
Their own heads are filled to bursting
with stupid concepts, so they try to relieve
the pressure by forcing you to choke down
their lunacy. Resist! Just say NO
to ridiculous ideas. If the Oddball persists,
tell it that Count Dracula wants to have sex
with a green toaster oven next September.
With any luck, that comment will make
the Oddball's flimsy brain
explode.

96.

The Cheerful Chirper

The Cheerful Chirper thinks that you – yes,
YOU, Mr. and/or Mrs. Joe/Josephine America –
are a super-rad coworker! It believes,
quite sincerely, that YOU rock so hard,
it hurts! The Cheerful Chirper also thinks that:
squirrels are neat, babies are da bomb,
wool is a groovy fabric, carpets are awesome,
pencils should be elected president of ancient Rome,
gravity is simply THE BEST (no two ways about it!),
and puppies and kittens are bliss times thirty-five!
What can I say?
The Cheerful Chirper is easily impressed.

97.

The Brainless Dawdler

Is the legendary Brainless Dawdler
truly brainless? Well, let's see.
It spent the last ninety-seven minutes
sweeping an empty storage room thirteen times.
Yep, that's some serious, industrial strength
dawdling. Even Dawdelus, the Greek god
of dawdling, didn't dawdle THAT much!
Truly, the Brainless Dawdler IS
the undisputed King of Dawdling.
So, let us raise our glasses – and then
set them back down again, because
we've forgotten where, when and who we are.
Is this seat taken?

98.

The Snore Bore

It wants to tell you so much
about so little. Listen and you shall hear
how its pet cat Pickles ate a ladybug
last Thursday, right after the Channel 7
weather report. As if any human on Earth
could possibly care. On and on
it will incessantly blather. Did you know,
Kansas gets really cold in winter?
Wow, there's a shocker. Stop the presses!
Just listening to the Snore Bore
makes you want to strangle it to death.
But fortunately for this tedious monster,
it will bore you into a deeeeep sleeeeep
before you can squeeze
its windpipe shut.

99.

The Mirrorgazing Megalomaniac

It feels pretty, oh so pretty…
pretty full of itself, that is.
This conceited creature loves to stare
into the delicious depths
of the nearest reflective surface.
It simply adores its own face.
If you have a coffee-break chat
with the beast, it will quickly
change the topic to (no big surprise)
itself. So please, don't ask the creature
out on a date. For in the mirror,
it has already found
its perfect mate.

100.

The Nicotine Nightmare

See how it greedily sucks
on its unfiltered coffin nails
in the alley outside the fire exit
during breaks. It puffs and wheezes
like a vile human locomotive,
heading down the long smoky tracks
of sickness and doom. Each slender
cancer-stick brings it a smidgen closer
to a breathless death. But hey,
we all have our sick obsessions,
our dirty, wicked, disgusting sins.
Drugs. Porn. Booze. And the worst,
the very worst of all…
Horror poems.

About the Authors

Michael McCarty has been a professional writer since 1983 and is the author of numerous books of fiction and nonfiction, as well as hundreds of articles, short stories, and poems. In 2009, he was named as a finalist, along with collaborator Mark McLaughlin, in two different Bram Stoker Award categories: Best First Novel of 2008 for Monster Behind the Wheel and Best Poetry Collection of 2008 for Attack of the Two-Headed Poetry Monster. He also received the 2008 David R. Collins Literary Achievement Award from the Midwest Writing Center. In 2005, he was a Bram Stoker Award finalist in the nonfiction category for More Giants of the Genre.

In late 2008, Lachesis Publishing released Michael's second novel, Out of Time, cowritten with Connie Corcoran Wilson. Other recent books are the satirical vampire novel, Liquid Diet, and the nonfiction collections, Esoteria-Land and Masters of Imagination.

Michael's fiction collections include Dark Duets, All Things Dark & Hideous, cowritten with Mark McLaughlin, Little Creatures, A Little Help from My Fiends, and Partners in Slime, also cowritten with Mark McLaughlin. His nonfiction books include Conversations with Kreskin, Giants of the Genre, and Modern Mythmakers.

In 2009, Darkside Digital released Professor LaGungo's Delirious Download of Digital Deviltry & Doom, an e-chapbook by Mark McLaughlin and McCarty. In 2010, Sam's Dot Publishing released Rusty the Robot's Holiday Adventures, a children's book by McCarty and Sherry Decker. In 2011, Bucket o' Guts Press released McLaughlin and McCarty's print chapbook, Professor LaGungo's Classroom of Horrors.

McCarty invites readers to visit him at www.Facebook.com/MichaelMcCartyMedia. He can be contacted at P.O. Box 4441, Rock Island, IL 61201, or by e-mail, darkduets@gmail.com.

Mark McLaughlin's fiction, nonfiction, and poetry have appeared in more than 1,000 magazines, newspapers, websites, and anthologies, including Cemetery Dance, Living Dead 2, Black Gate, Galaxy, Fangoria, Writer's Digest, Midnight Premiere, Dark Arts, In Laymon's Terms, and two volumes each of The Best of HorrorFind and The Year's Best Horror Stories (DAW Books).

Collections of McLaughlin's fiction include Beach Blanket Zombie, Best Little Witch-House in Arkham, Motivational Shrieker, Slime After Slime, Pickman's Motel, and Raising Demons for Fun and Profit. He is the coauthor of At the Foothills of Frenzy with coauthors Shane Ryan Staley and Brian Knight. Also, McLaughlin is the coauthor, with Rain Graves and David Niall Wilson, of The Gossamer Eye, which won the 2002 Bram Stoker Award for Superior Achievement in Poetry.

With regular collaborator Michael McCarty, he has written Monster Behind the Wheel, Attack of the Two-Headed Poetry Monster, All Things Dark & Hideous, Professor LaGungo's Delirious Download of Digital Deviltry & Doom, Professor LaGungo's Classroom of Horrors, and Partners in Slime.

HorrorGarage.com features his online column, Four-Letter Word Beginning with 'F' (the word in question is Fear). GravesideTales.com is the home of his blog, Time Machine of Terror! An expert on B-movies, he was once interviewed by an AOL columnist about Gamera's place in cinematic history. He is also a successful marketing and public relations executive who writes articles for business journals, newspapers, trade publications and websites.

You can befriend McLaughlin at www.Facebook.com/MarkMcLaughlinMedia. Be sure to visit his Amazon.com Author's Page at www.amazon.com/author/markmclaughlinmedia. Also, you can read his horror/B-movie blog at www.BMovieMonster.com.

Acknowledgments

Previously Published:

Michael McCarty:
Psycho Woman in My Shower, Nasty Piece of Work #11 (UK), 1999
Frankenfrog, Indigenous Fiction #3, 1999
Dusk (with R.L. Fox), Goddess of the Bay #4, 1998
Not One of Us and Requiem, Requiem #1, 1999
Ich and My Cannibal Girlfriend, The Urbanite #11, 1999
The Troll of Madison County, Son of Wyatt Earp Battles the Aztec Mummy (with Cindy McCarty), The Road to Hell, Making Out with Kali, Dangerous, The Pet Exorcist, Of Thee I Sing, The Word, Somebody's Knocking, Slimy Creatures from Outer Space Introduction, Alien Prisoner (with Sandy DeLuca), Crop Circles, Cute, Cuddly Creatures from Another Planet, Gone Hollywood, Illegal Aliens, Area 51, Where are You?, The Others (with Sandy DeLuca), Alien Anal Probe, MIB, MIB II, War of the Worlds, It Came from Uranus, Beyond the Moonlight (with Terrie Leigh Relf), Succubus, Vampire's Kiss, Vegas Undead, Sex with a Vampire, and Television all appeared in Attack of the Two-Headed Poetry Monster by Mark McLaughlin & Michael McCarty, Skullvines Press, 2008.

Mark McLaughlin:
Cinema Diabolique, Cyber-Psycho's AOD #8, 1998.
Big is Beautiful, Men are from Hell, Women are from the Galaxy of Death by Mark McLaughlin, Kelp Queen Press, 2004
What the Sorceress with a Sweet Tooth Had to Say to the Angry Mob Before They Cut Out Her Tongue, Underworlds, December 2004.
Cleopatrick, Isis Rising, 2000.
The Spiderweb Tree, Hansel & Gristle, Ratpunzel, Horror House of Thumb, Saved from a Grizzly Demise, Wicked Queen, Ashley, Joe White, Loved Her, Hated Him, Kiss, and Stalked appeared in The Spiderweb Tree by Mark McLaughlin, Yellow Bat Press, 2003.
I Am the Monster's Naval, I Am the Monster's Heart, I Am the Monster's Penis, I Am the Monster's Fifth Kidney, I Am the Monster's Right Knee, I Am the Monster's Left Ear, I Am the Monster's Bottom Lip, I Am the Monster's Pinky, I Am the Monster's Stomach, I Am the Monster's Hazel Eye, I Am the Monster's Thumb, I Am the Monster's Sphincter, and I Am the Monster's Brain appeared in The Gossamer Eye by Mark McLaughlin,

Rain Graves and David Niall Wilson, Meisha Merlin, 2002.
The Enthusiraptor, The Fumigorgon, The Normitron, The Smiling Gladhander, The Waffler, The Spittylicker, The Blabberblort, The Potbellied Smirkleflab, The Zitastrophee, The Finicky Foofoo, The Screaming Snotty, and The Caterwauler appeared in Your Handy Office Guide to Corporate Monsters by Mark McLaughlin, Yellow Bat Press, 2002.

Michael McCarty and Mark McLaughlin:
Zombie Insomniacs and Orange Demon in My Brain appeared in Attack of the Two-Headed Poetry Monster by Mark McLaughlin & Michael McCarty, Skullvines Press, 2008.

Unpublished:

Professor Artemis Theodore LaGungo:
Introduction: No Bawdy Rhymes for Nantucket in THIS Book of Poetry, Thank You Very Much!

Michael McCarty:
Frosty the Serial Killer Snowman, The Old House on the Corner (with Terrie Leigh Relf), Zombie Jack Spratt, Jack Be Dinner, and Old Mother Hubbard's Kennel of Blood.

Mark McLaughlin:
Electric Charity Begins at Home, The Storyteller Out of Time, Rotted Hearts Ought Not to Pulse, Nyarlathenstein, Cthulhu's Daughter, Pickman's Werewolf, and The Colour from the Blasted Lagoon.

Mark McLaughlin and Michael McCarty:
The Backstabbing Narkalope, The Slothazoid, The Belligerent Brag-Hag, The Office Oddball, The Cheerful Chirper, The Brainless Dawdler, The Snore Bore, The Mirrorgazing Megalomaniac and The Nicotine Nightmare.